BREAK OF DAY

"What delights and endears in *Break of Day* is, as always, Colette's precise, tender, enchanted description of sensuous pleasure: the love she feels for a shrub cosily settled in the moist earth, the sour scent of peaches, her hand on the young man's beautiful brown chest: this is incomparable writing, even in translation."
The Times Literary Supplement

Also by Colette
Published by Ballantine Books:

THE VAGABOND

THE SHACKLE

CHERI AND THE LAST OF CHERI

CLAUDINE AT SCHOOL

CLAUDINE IN PARIS

CLAUDINE MARRIED/CLAUDINE AND ANNIE

Colette

BREAK
OF DAY

Translated by Enid McLeod

BALLANTINE BOOKS • NEW YORK

Library of Congress Catalog Card Number: 61-17502

ISBN 0-345-30858-1

This edition published by arrangement with Farrar, Straus and
Giroux, Inc.

Manufactured in the United States of America

First Ballantine Books Edition: June 1983

"Are you imagining, as you read me,
that I'm portraying myself?
Have patience: this is merely my model."

Sir,

"You ask me to come and spend a week with you, which means I would be near my daughter, whom I adore. You who live with her know how rarely I see her, how much her presence delights me, and I'm touched that you should ask me to come and see her. All the same I'm not going to accept your kind invitation, for the time being at any rate. The reason is that my pink cactus is probably going to flower. It's a very rare plant I've been given, and I'm told that in our climate it flowers only once every four years. Now, I am already a very old woman, and if I went away when my pink catus is about to flower, I am certain I shouldn't see it flower again.

"So I beg you, Sir, to accept my sincere thanks and my regrets, together with my kind regards."

This note, signed *"Sidonie Colette, née Landoy"*, was written by my mother to one of my husbands, the second. A year later she died, at the age of seventy-seven.

Whenever I feel myself inferior to everything about me, threatened by my own mediocrity, frightened by the discovery that a muscle is losing its strength, a desire its power or a pain the keen edge of its bite, I can still hold up my head and say to myself: "I am the

1

daughter of the woman who wrote that letter—that letter and so many more that I have kept. This one tells me in ten lines that at the age of seventy-six she was planning journeys and undertaking them, but that waiting for the possible bursting into bloom of a tropical flower held everything up and silenced even her heart, made for love. I am the daughter of a woman who, in a mean, close-fisted, confined little place, opened her village home to stray cats, tramps and pregnant servant-girls. I am the daughter of a woman who many a time, when she was in despair at not having enough money for others, ran through the wind-whipped snow to cry from door to door, at the houses of the rich, that a child had just been born in a poverty-stricken home to parents whose feeble, empty hands had no swaddling clothes for it. Let me not forget that I am the daughter of a woman who bent her head, trembling, between the blades of a cactus, her wrinkled face full of ecstasy over the promise of a flower, a woman who herself never ceased to flower, untiringly, during three quarters of a century."

Now that little by little I am beginning to age, and little by little taking on her likeness in the mirror, I wonder whether, if she were to return, she would recognise me for her daughter, in spite of the resemblance of our features. She might if she came back at break of day and found me up and alert in a sleeping world, awake as she used to be, and I often am, before everyone.

Before almost everyone, O my chaste, serene ghost! But you wouldn't find me in a blue apron with pockets full of grain for the fowls, nor with secateurs or a wooden pail. Up before almost everyone, but half-naked in a fluttering wrap hastily slipped on, standing at my door which had admitted a nightly visitor, my arms trembling with passion and shielding—let me hide myself for shame!—the shadow, the thin shadow of a man.

"Stand aside and let me see," my beloved ghost would

say. "Why, isn't what you're embracing my pink cactus, that has survived me? How amazingly it's grown and changed! But now that I look into your face, my child, I recognise it. I recognise it by your agitation, by your air of waiting, by the devotion in your outspread hands, by the beating of your heart and your suppressed cry, by the growing daylight all about you, yes, I recognise, I lay claim to all of that. Stay where you are, don't hide, and may you both be left in peace, you and the man you're embracing, for I see that he is in truth my pink cactus, that has at last consented to flower."

Is THIS HOUSE GOING TO BE MY LAST? I WEIGH IT UP
and listen to it during that short private night that en-
wraps us, here in the Midi, immediately after the hour
of noon. The cicadas creak and so does the new wattle
fencing that shelters the terrace, a nameless insect is
crushing tiny grits between its shards, the reddish bird
in the pine tree calls every ten seconds, and the west
wind, circling watchfully round my walls, leaves un-
ruffled the flat, dense, hard sea, whose harsh blue will
soften towards nightfall.

Is this house going to be my last, the one that will
find me faithful, the one I shall never leave again? It is
so ordinary that it could have no rivals.

I hear the clink of the bottles being carried to the
well from which they will be pulled up, cooled, for
dinner to-night. One of them, red-currant pink, will
accompany the green melon; the other, a sand-grown
wine, amber-coloured and over-generous, goes with the
salad of tomatoes, pimentos and onions soaked in oil,
and with the ripe fruit. After dinner I mustn't forget to
irrigate the little runnels that surround the melons, and
to water by hand the balsams, phlox and dahlias, and
the young tangerine trees, which haven't yet got roots
long enough to drink unaided in the depths of the earth,
nor strength to break into leaf without help, under the
steady scorching of the heavens. The young tangerine
trees, planted . . . for whom? I don't know. Perhaps for

4

me. The cats will spring sideways at the moths when by ten the air is blue as a morning glory. The pair of Japanese hens, perching drowsily on the arm of a rustic armchair, will chirp like birds in a nest. The dogs, already far away from this world, will be thinking of the coming dawn, and I shall have the choice of a book, bed, or the coast road studded with fluting toads.

To-morrow I shall surprise the red dawn on the tamarisks wet with salty dew, and on the mock bamboos where a pearl hangs at the tip of each blue lance. The coast road that leads up from the night, the mist and the sea; then a bath, work and rest. How simple everything could be! Can it be that I have attained here what one never starts a second time? Everything is much as it was in the first years of my life, and little by little I recognise the road back. The way my country house has grown smaller, the cats, the aged bitch, my sense of wonder and a serenity whose breath I can feel from far off—a merciful moisture, a promise of healing rain hanging over my still-stormy life—all these help me to recognise it. Many stretches of the road have been completed and left behind. A castle inhabited for a moment has melted into the distance, replaced by this little house. Properties scattered over France have dwindled little by little in response to a wish that in times past I never dared to put into words. How wonderfully confident and vital must that past have been to inspire even the lowly guardian angels of the present: the servitors who have once again become humble and competent. The housemaid adores digging and the cook soaps the linen in the wash-house. Does there then exist here on earth a kitchen-garden path where I can retrace my own footsteps, a path I thought I should never follow again except on the other side of life? Is that maternal ghost, in the old-fashioned dress of blue sateen, filling the watering-cans on the edge of the well? This coolness of spray, this sweet enticement, this provincial spirit, in short this innocence, isn't all this the charm of declining years? How simple everything has become!

Everything, even to the second place that I sometimes lay opposite my own on the shady table.

A second place doesn't take much room now: a green plate, a thick antique glass, slightly cloudy. If I say that it is to be taken away for good, no pernicious blast will blow suddenly from the horizon to make my hair stand on end and alter the direction of my life, as once it did. If that place is removed from my table I shall still eat with appetite. There is no longer any mystery, no longer a serpent coiled under the napkin ringed, to distinguish it from mine, with a brass lyre which once held in place, at the top of a music-stand of the last century, the loose pages of a score where only the down-beats were marked, spaced at intervals as regular as tears. This place belongs to the friend who comes and goes, and no longer to a master of the house given to treading the resounding boards of a bedroom up above during the night. On days when the plate, the glass and the lyre are not in front of me, I am merely alone, and not abandoned. Now that my friends are reassured about that, they trust me.

Very few, only two or three, remain of those friends who in former days thought they saw me going under in my first shipwreck: for I honestly thought so myself and said as much to them. To these, one by one, death is bringing rest. I have friends who are younger, and in particular younger than I. I instinctively like to acquire and store up what looks like outlasting me. I have not caused such great torments to these, at most a few cares: "There now, *He's* going to spoil her for us again. . . . How long is *He* going to remain so important?" They would speculate on the outcome of the disease, its crises and its temperature chart: "A dangerous typhoid or a mild rash? Confound the woman, why does she always manage to catch such serious complaints!" My true friends have always given me that supreme proof of devotion, a spontaneous aversion for the man I loved. "And what if this one disappears too, what a lot of trouble it will give us, what a job to help her recover her balance!"

But at bottom they never grumbled greatly—very much the other way—when they saw me coming back to them overheated by the struggle, licking my wounds, counting my tactical errors, revelling in being biased, heaping crimes on the enemy who defies me, then whitewashing him out of all measure, then secretly hugging his letters and pictures: "He was charming . . . I ought to have . . . I ought not to have . . ." Then reason would return, bringing with it the calm that I do not like and my belatedly courteous, belatedly reserved silence which is, I really believe, the worst moment of all. Such is the routine of suffering, like the habitual clumsiness of those in love, and the compulsion which makes every couple innocently poison their home life.

Then is that militant life, that I thought I should never see the last of, over and done with? I have nothing left now but my dreams with which to revive from time to time a dead love, by which I mean love purged of its brief and localised pleasures. Sometimes it happens that in a dream one of my loves begins again with an indescribable noise, a tumult of words, of looks that can be interpreted in two or three contradictory ways, of demands. Without any break or transition, the same dream ends in an exam in decimal fractions for the lower certificate. And if when I wake the pillow under the nape of my neck is a bit damp, it is because of the lower certificate. "A second longer and I should have failed in the oral," stammers memory, still caught in the toils. "Ah, that look he had in my dream! Who? The highest common factor? No, of course not, He, He when he used to spy on me through the window, to see if I had deceived him. But it wasn't He, it was . . . was it?" The light mounts, forcibly enlarging the gilded green field of vision between my eyelids. "Was it He, or else . . . ? I'm sure it's at least seven o'clock—if it's seven it's too late to water the aubergines—the sun is

on them. And why, before I woke, didn't I brandish
under his nose that letter in which he promised me
peace, friendship, a better mutual knowledge of ourselves and . . . it's the first time I've got up so late this
whole season." For to dream, and then to return to
reality, only means that our scruples suffer a change of
place and significance.

A little wing of light is beating between the two
shutters, touching with irregular pulsations the wall or
the long heavy table where we write or read or play,
that eternal table that has come back from Brittany,
as I have come back. Sometimes the wing of light is
pink on the pink-washed wall, and sometimes blue on
the blue cotton Moroccan rug. Dressers stacked with
books, armchairs and chests of drawers have made a
roundabout journey with me over fifteen years, through
two or three French provinces. Elegant armchairs with
tapering arms, countrified like peasant girls with delicate
limbs, yellow plates that sing like bells when you rub
them with your finger, dishes of thick white glaze—
we are all astonished to find ourselves back in a country
that is our own. For is not the house of my father and
my grandparents on the Mourillon, fifty miles from
here? It is true that other regions have cradled me, and
some of them roughly. A woman lays claim to as many
native lands as she has had happy loves. She is born,
too, under every sky where she had recovered from the
pain of loving. By that reckoning this blue salt shore,
bright with tomatoes and pimentos, is doubly mine.
How rich it is, and what a lot of time I've spent not
knowing of it! The air is light, the grapes ripen so
quickly that they are dried and wrinkled on the vine by
the sun, the garlic is highly flavoured. That noble bareness that thirst sometimes confers on the soil, the re-
fined idleness that one learns from a frugal people—for
me these are late-discovered riches. But let me not com-
plain. My maturity is the right time for them. My angular

youth would have bled at the touch of the striated, mica-spangled rocks, the forked pine-needles, the agave, the spines of the sea-urchin, the bitter, sticky cistus and the fig tree, the underside of whose every leaf is a wild beast's tongue. What a country! The invader endows it with villas and garages, with motor-cars and dance-halls built to look like *Mas*. The barbarians from the north parcel out the land, speculate and deforest, and that is certainly a great pity. But during the course of the centuries how many ravishers have not fallen in love with such a captive? They arrive plotting to ruin her, stop suddenly and listen to her breathing in her sleep, and then, turning silent and respectful, they softly shut the gate in the fence. Submissive to your wishes, Provence, they fasten on your vine-leaf crown again, replant the pine tree and the fig, sow the variegated melon and have no other desire, Beauty, than to serve you and enjoy it.

The others will inevitably abandon you. Once upon a time they would have dishonoured you. But one horde more or less doesn't matter to you. Those who have come on the strength of a casino, an hotel or a post-card will leave you. They will flee, burnt and bitten by your wind white with dust. Keep your lovers, who drink water from the pitcher and the dry wine that ripens in the sand; keep those who pour oil religiously and turn away their heads when they pass in front of dead animals; keep those who rise early and lull themselves asleep in bed in the evening to the faint chugging of the pleasure-boats in the bay. Keep me. . . .

The ripening colour of the half-light marks the end of my siesta. The prostrate cat will now for a certainty stretch herself to a phenomenal length, produce from her body a front paw whose exact length no one knows, and say, with a yawn like a flower: "It's long past four o'clock." The first motor-car is not far off, rolling on its little cloud of dust towards the shore; others will follow it. One of them will stop for a moment at the gate, and out of it there will pour on to the path, amid the feathery shade of the mimosas, men-friends without their wives and women-friends with their lovers. I haven't yet got to the point of shutting my gate in their faces and baring my teeth behind it. But the tone of my cordiality, familiar but cold, does not deceive them, and keeps them in check. The men like my dwelling, without a master; they like its smell, its doors with no locks. Some of the women say, with an air of sudden ecstasy: "Oh, what a paradise!" and secretly tot up all it lacks. But both the women and the men appreciate the patience with which I, who have no projects of my own, listen to theirs. They are "mad about this country", they want "a very simple little farm", or to build "a *mas* on this headland above the sea, by Jove, what a view!" At that point I become charming because I listen and say: "Yes, yes." For I do not covet the field alongside, I am not buying my neighbour's vineyard, and I'm not "adding a wing". There's always one of my comrades who eyes my vines, walks from the house to the sea without going up or down a step, returns and concludes: "The long and the short of it is that this property, just as it is, suits you perfectly."

And I say "Yes, yes", as I do when he or someone else assures me: "You don't change!", which means: "We've made up our minds that you never will change any more."

I'd very much like to try once again.

THE DOOR LEADING TO THE VINES FROM THE ENclosure walled with openwork bricks is straining slightly on its hinges; the wind must be rising. It will swiftly sweep a quarter of the horizon and fasten on the wintry purity of the greenish north. Thereupon the whole hollow of the bay will boom like a shell. Goodbye to my night in the open on the raffia mattress! If I had persisted in sleeping out of doors, that powerful mouth that breathes coldness and drought, deadens all scents and anaesthetises the earth, the enemy of work, voluptuousness and sleep, would have torn off me the sheets and blankets that it knows how to twist into long rolls. What a strange tormentor, as intent on man as any wild beast! Those who are highly strung know more about it than I do. My Provençal cook, when the wind strikes her near the well, puts down her buckets, holds her head and cries: "It's killing me!" On nights when the mistral blows she groans under it in her little hut among the vines, and perhaps she sees it.

Having retired to my bedroom I wait with controlled impatience for the departure of this visitor for whom no sanctum is private, and who is already pushing under my door a strange tribute of withered petals, finely sifted seeds, sand and battered butterflies. Be off with you, I've discouraged other tokens before now; and I'm no longer forty, to avert my eyes at sight of a fading rose. Is that militant life over and done with then? There

11

are three good times for thinking of it: the siesta, a short hour after dinner when the rustling of the newspaper, just arrived from Paris, seems oddly to fill the room, and then the irregular insomnia of the small hours, before dawn. Yes, it will soon be three o'clock. But even during these precarious small hours, that merge so quickly into day, where can I find that great cavern of bitterness promised me by my past griefs and joys, as well as my own books and those of others? Humble as I always am when I'm faced with anything I don't understand, I'm afraid of being mistaken when I imagine that this is the beginning of a long rest between myself and men. Come, Man, my friend, let us simply exist side by side! I have always liked your company. Just now you're looking at me so gently. What you see emerging from a confused heap of feminine cast-offs, still weighed down like a drowned woman by seaweed (for even if my head is saved, I cannot be sure that my struggling body will be), is your sister, your comrade: a woman who is escaping from the age when she is a woman. She has, like you, rather a thick neck, bodily strength that becomes less graceful as it weakens, and that authority which shows you that you can no longer make her despair, or only dispassionately. Let us remain together; you no longer have any reasons now for saying goodbye to me for ever.

Love, one of the great commonplaces of existence, is slowly leaving mine. The maternal instinct is another great commonplace. Once we've left these behind, we find that all the rest is gay and varied, and that there is plenty of it. But one doesn't leave all that behind when or as one pleases. How wise one of my husbands was when he remonstrated: "But is it impossible for you to write a book that isn't about love, adultery, semi-incestuous relations and a final separation? Aren't there other things in life?" If he had not been in such a hurry to get to his amorous rendezvous—for he was handsome and charming—he might perhaps have taught me what can take the place of love, in a novel or out of it. But he went and I continued obstinately covering that same bluish paper, gleaming at this moment from the dark table to guide my hand, with chapters dedicated to love or regret for love, chapters blind with love. In them I called myself Renée Néré or else, prophetically, I introduced a Léa. So it came about that both legally and familiarly, as well as in my books, I now have only one name, which is my own. Did it take only thirty years of my life to reach that point, or rather to get back to it? I shall end by thinking that it wasn't too high a price to pay. Can it be that chance has made me one of those women so immersed in one man that, whether they are barren or not, they carry with them to the grave the shrivelled innocence of an old maid? At the thought of such a fate my plump double that I see in the sloping mirror, tanned by sun and sea, would tremble, if it could still tremble at a past danger.

A hawk-moth from the oleanders is banging against the fine wire-netting in front of the French window, returning to the charge again and again until the taut netting reverberates like the skin of a drum. It is cool. The generous dew trickles, the mistral has put off its offensive. The stars, magnified by the damp and salty air, twinkle broadly. Once again the most beautiful of all nights precedes the most beautiful of all days, and not being asleep, I can enjoy it. Let us hope to-morrow will find me equally sweet-tempered! In all sincerity I no longer ask for anything except what I can't have. Has someone broken my spirit, that I should be so gentle? Not at all: it's a very long time since I knew anyone really wicked—knew them face to face, bosom to bosom and limb to limb. As for an authentic villain, the real thing, the absolute, the artist, one rarely meets him even once in a lifetime. The ordinary bad hat is always in part a decent fellow. It's true that the third hour of the morning encourages indulgence in those who enjoy it in the open and have an assignation with no one but themselves beneath the deepening blue of their window. The crystalline emptiness of the sky, the already conscious sleep of the animals, the chilly contraction that closes the calyxes up again, are so many antidotes to passion and iniquity. But I don't need to be feeling indulgent in order to say that in my past no one has broken my spirit. I was made to suffer, oh yes, certainly I learnt how to suffer. But is suffering so very serious? I have come to doubt it. It may be quite childish, a sort of undignified pastime—I'm referring to the kind of suffering a man inflicts on a woman or a woman on a man. It's extremely painful. I agree that it's hardly bearable. But I very much fear that this sort of pain deserves no consideration at all. It's no more worthy of respect than old age or illness, for both of which I'm acquiring a great repulsion: both of them are anxious to get me in their clutches before long, and I'm holding my nose in advance. The love-sick, the betrayed and the jealous all smell alike.

I remember very definitely that when I was wretched because I had been disappointed in love, my animals loved me less. They scented my grief, that great admission of failure. I have seen an unforgettable look in the eyes of a beautiful well-bred bitch, a look still generous but restrained and politely bored, because she no longer loved as much all that I stood for—a man's look, the look of a certain man. Shall we never have done with that cliché, so stupid that it could only be human, about the sympathy of animals for man when he is unhappy? Animals love happiness almost as much as we do. A fit of crying disturbs them, they'll sometimes imitate sobbing, and for a moment they'll reflect our sadness. But they flee unhappiness as they flee fever, and I believe that in the long run they are capable of boycotting it.

What a good use the two tom-cats fighting outside are making of the July night! Those unearthly songs of the male cat have accompanied so many nocturnal hours in my life that they have become a symbol of wakefulness, of ritual insomnia. Yes, I know it is three o'clock and that I'm going to fall asleep again, and that when I wake I shall be sorry to have missed the moment when the milky blueness begins to rise up from the sea, reaches the sky and flows over it until it stops at a red rift flush with the horizon.

The great voice of a baritone wild beast, long drawn out, persists through the sharp sounds of a tenor cat, clever at tremolos and at shrill chromatic scales interrupted by furious innuendoes growing more nasal the more insulting they become. The two tom-cats do not hate each other, but the clear nights suggest battle and declamatory dialogues. Why sleep? They make their choice and in summer take only the best parts of the night and the day. They choose. All animals who are well treated choose whatever is best in us and in their surroundings. It was the realisation of that that helped me to emerge from the period when their comparative coldness revealed to me my own lack of dignity. I choose the phrase, lack of dignity, advisedly. Surely I ought to have thrown off that sordid domination? It was all in such deplorable taste, those half-dried tears, that melodrama. What opinion of a woman like that could one expect from an animal, a bitch for instance, herself compact of hidden fire and secrets, a bitch who had never groaned under the whip or wept in public? She despised me, that goes without saying. And though I didn't hide my hurt from the eyes of my fellows, I blushed for it in her presence. It is true that she and I loved the same man. But for all that it was in her eyes that I read a thought that I've read in one of my mother's last letters: "Love is not a sentiment worthy of respect."

One of my husbands used to suggest to me: "When you're about fifty you ought to write a sort of handbook to teach women how to live in peace with the man they love, a code for life as a couple." Perhaps I am writing it now. O Man, my former loves, how one gains and learns in your company! Yet the best of friends must part; but I pledge myself here to take my leave courteously. No, you have not broken me, perhaps you never meant me any harm. Farewell, dear Man, and welcome to you too. Across my bed which, since I am in good health, is better arranged for writing than a sick bed, a blue light creeps until it reaches the blue paper, my hand and my bronze-coloured arm; the smell of the sea warns me that the hour when air is colder than water is at hand. Shall I get up? To sleep is sweet.

There is about a very beautiful child something I can't define which makes me sad. How can I make myself clear? Your little niece C. is at this moment ravishingly beautiful. Full face she's still nothing much, but when she turns her profile in a certain way and you see the proud outline of her pure little nose below her lovely lashes, I am seized with an admiration that somehow disturbs me. They say that great lovers feel like that before the object of their passion. Can it be then that, in my way, I am a great lover? That's a discovery that would much have astonished my two husbands!"

So she was able, was she, to bend over a human flower with no harm to herself, no harm save for that "sadness"; was sadness her word for that melancholy ecstasy, that sense of exaltation which uplifts us when we see the waxen purity of faces dissolving into an arabesque never resembling its original, never twice the same: the dual fires of the eyes, the nostrils like twin calyxes, the little sea-cave of the mouth quivering as it waits for its prey? When she bent over a glorious childish creature she would tremble and sigh, seized with an anguish she could not explain, whose name is temptation. For it would never have occurred to her that from a youthful face there could emanate a perturbation, a mist like that which floats above grapes in their vat, nor that one could succumb to it. My first communings with myself taught me the lesson, though I failed to observe it sometimes: "Never touch a butterfly's wing with your finger."

"I certainly won't . . . or only just lightly . . . just at the tawny-black place where you see that violet glow, that moon-lick, without being able to say exactly where it starts or where it dies away."

"No, don't touch it. The whole thing will vanish if you merely brush it."

"But only just lightly! Perhaps this will be the time when I shall feel under this particular finger, my fourth, the most sensitive, the cold blue flame and the way it vanishes into the skin of the wing—the feathers of the wing—the dew of the wing . . ." A trace of lifeless ash on the tip of my finger, the wing dishonoured, the tiny creature weakened.

There is no doubt that my mother, who only learned, as she said, "by getting burnt", knew that one possesses through abstaining, and only through abstaining. For a "great lover" of her sort—of our sort—there is not much difference between the sin of abstention and that of consummation. Serene and gay in the presence of her husband, she became disturbed, and distracted with an unexplained passion when she came in contact with someone who was passing through a sublime experience. Confined to her village by her two successive husbands and four children, she had the power of conjuring up everywhere unexpected crises, burgeonings, metamorphoses and dramatic miracles, which she herself provoked and whose value she savoured to the full. She who nursed animals, cared for children and looked after plants, was spared the discovery that some creatures want to die, that certain children long to be defiled, that one of the buds is determined to be forced open and then trampled underfoot. Her form of inconstancy was to fly from the bee to the mouse, from a new-born child to a tree, from a poor person to a poorer, from laughter to torment. How pure are those who lavish themselves in this way! In her life there was never the memory of a dishonoured wing, and if she trembled with longing in the presence of a closed calyx, a chrysalis still rolled in its varnished cocoon, at least she respectfully awaited the moment. How pure are those who have never forced anything open! To bring my mother close to me again I have to think back to those dramatic dreams she dreamt throughout the adolescence of her elder son, who was so beautiful and so seductive. At that time I was aware that she was wild, full of false gaiety, given to maledictions, ordinary, plain-looking and on the alert. Oh, if only I could see her again thus diminished, her cheeks flushed red with jealousy and rage! If only I could see her thus, and could she but understand me well enough to recognise herself in what she would most strongly have reproved! If only I, grown wise in my turn, could show her how much her own image, though coarsened and impure, survives in me, her faithful servant, whose job is the menial tasks! She gave me life and the mission to pursue those things which she, a poet, seized and cast aside as one snatches a fragment of a floating melody drifting through space. What does the melody matter to one whose concern is the bow and the hand that holds the bow?

She pursued her innocent ends with increasing anxiety. She rose early, then earlier, then earlier still. She wanted to have the world to herself, deserted, in the form of a little enclosure with a trellis and a sloping roof. She wanted the jungle to be virgin, but even so inhabited only by swallows, cats and bees, and the huge spider balancing atop his wheel of lace silvered by the night. The neighbour's shutter, banging against the wall, spoilt her dream of being an unchallengeable explorer, a dream repeated every day at the hour when the cold dew seems to be falling, with little irregular plops, from the beaks of the blackbirds. She got up at six, then at five, and at the end of her life a little red lamp wakened her, in winter, long before the angelus smote the black air.

In those moments while it was still night my mother used to sing, falling silent as soon as anyone was able to hear. The lark also sings while it is mounting towards the palest, least inhabited part of the sky. My mother climbed too, mounting ceaselessly up the ladder of the hours, trying to possess the beginning of the beginning. I know what that particular intoxication is like. But what she sought was a red, horizontal ray, and the pale sulphur that comes before the red ray; she wanted the damp wing that the first bee stretches out like an arm. The summer wind, that springs up at the approach of the sun, gave her its first-fruits in scents of acacia and woodsmoke; when a horse pawed the ground and whinnied softly in the neighbouring stable, she was the first to hear it. On an autumn morning she was the only one to see herself reflected in the first disk of ephemeral ice in the well-bucket, before her nail cracked it.

How I wish I could have put before that hard and convex nail, made for cutting stalks, plucking scented leaves, scraping off greenfly and questioning seeds sleeping in the earth, how I wish I could have put before it my own mirror of long ago: that tender face, so little virile, that gave me back my own image beautified! I would have said to my mother: "Look. See what I'm doing. Measure what it's worth. Is it worth my assuming a tarnished reputation in order to nourish in secret, mouth to mouth, the prey that people think I am myself absorbing? Is it worth my turning away from those dawns that you and I love, to give myself to eyelids that I dazzle and their promises of stardom? Judge, better than I can, my hesitant work that I've gazed at too much. Trim your hard gardener's nail!" But it was too late. By the time I confessed all that to her she had already attained her everlasting morning twilight. She would, alas, have judged us plainly, with that divine cruelty of hers which was innocent of wrath. "Pluck off that rather unnatural shoot of yours, my daughter, that graft that doesn't want to thrive except on you. It's a mistletoe. I assure you it's a mistletoe. I'm not saying to you that it's a bad thing to take on a mistletoe, because evil and good can be equally resplendent and fruitful. But . . ."

When I try to invent what she would have said to me, there is always one place at which I falter. I lack the words, above all the essential argument, the unexpected and equally enchanting blame and indulgence which fell from her so lightly, slow to touch and gently penetrate my clay, and then come to the surface again. Now they well up in what I write and sometimes they are thought beautiful. But I know well that, though recognisable, they are deformed by my personal notions, my limited unselfishness, my half-hearted generosity and my sensuality whose eyes, thank God, were always bigger than its belly.

Each of us had two husbands, but whereas both of mine—I'm glad to say—are very much alive, my mother was twice a widow. Since she was faithful out of tenderness, duty and pride, my first divorce upset her greatly and my second marriage still more. Her odd explanation of this was: "It's not so much the divorce I mind, it's the marriage. It seems to me that anything would be better than marriage—only it isn't done." I laughed and pointed out that on two occasions she had set me an example. "I had to," she answered. "After all I belong to my village. But what are you going to do with so many husbands? It's a habit that grows and soon you won't be able to do without it."

"But Mother, what would you do in my place?"

"Something stupid, no doubt. The proof is that I married your father."

If she was afraid to say how great a place he had held in her heart, her letters, after he had left her for ever, told me of it, as did also an outburst of tears on the day after my father was buried. That day she and I were tidying the drawers of the yellow thuya-wood desk from which she took letters, the service records of

Jules-Joseph Colette, Captain of the First Regiment of
Zouaves, and six hundred gold francs—all that remained of a landed fortune, the fortune of Sidonie
Landoy, frittered away. My mother, who had shown no
signs of weakness as she moved about surrounded by
relics, came across this handful of gold, gave a cry,
melted into tears and said: "Oh, dear Colette! He'd told
me, eight days ago, when he could still speak to me, that
he was only leaving me four hundred francs!" She
sobbed with gratitude, and I began that day to doubt
whether I had ever truly loved. No, certainly, a woman
as great as that could not commit the same "stupidities"
as I, and she was the first to discourage me from imitat-
ing her:

"So this Monsieur X means a lot to you, does he?"

"But Mother, I love him!"

"Yes, yes, you love him. . . . All right then, you
love him."

She thought again, refrained with an effort from saying what her celestial cruelty dictated, then burst out
once more:

"No, no, I'm not happy."

I pretended to be modest, dropped my eyes to shut
in the image of a handsome, envied, intelligent man,
with a glowing future, and replied gently:

"You're difficult."

"No, I'm not happy. I preferred, yes really I preferred the other one, the boy you now consider less than
the dust."

"Oh Mother! He's an idiot!"

"Yes, yes, an idiot. . . . Exactly."

I still remember how she bent her head, half-closing
her grey eyes to dwell on the dazzling, flattering picture
of the "idiot". And she added: "What beautiful things
you'd write with the idiot, Minet-Chéri! With the other,
you'll spend your time giving him all your most precious gifts. And what if on top of that he makes you
unhappy? It's more than likely."

I laughed heartily: "Cassandra!"

"All right then, Cassandra. And if I were to say all I foresee . . ." The grey eyes, half-closed, read the future: "Fortunately you're not in too much danger."

At the time I did not understand her. No doubt she would have explained herself later on. I know now what she meant when she said "you're not in danger", an ambiguous phrase referring not only to the calamities I risked. To her mind I had already got over what she called "the worst thing in a woman's life: her first man". He is the only one you die of. After that, married life—or a semblance of it—becomes a career, and sometimes a system of bureaucratic rule in which the only thing that distracts us and takes us out of ourselves is that balancing trick which, at the appointed time, impels the greybeard towards the flapper, and Chéri towards Léa.

Then, in obedience to the law of the climacteric, we can at last triumph over what I will call the ordinary run of lovers, provided we don't let this become a sordid habit. But it is essential that this triumph should be born of a cataclysm, die in the same way, and not allowed to feed a contemptible regular hunger. Any love, no matter what, if one lets it have its way, tends to turn itself into a sort of alimentary canal, seizing every opportunity of losing its exceptional quality, its tormentor's nobility.

"Autumn is the only vintage time"—perhaps that is true in love too. It is the season for sensual affection, a time of truce in the monotonous succession of struggles between equals, the perfect time for resting on a summit where two slopes meet. Autumn is the only vintage time; and a mouth still stained with a purplish drop, like a dried tear, of a juice that was not yet the true wine, has the right to proclaim it. Oh the eager joy of vintage, the haste to cast into the winepress on the same day both the ripe grape and the verjuice, the rhythm which leaves far behind the ample, dreamy cadence of harvest, the pleasure, redder than other pleasures, the songs and drunken shouts! Then silence, withdrawal, the sleep of the new wine sealed up, re-moved from those stained hands that did it violence! It pleases me to think that hearts and bodies suffer a similar fate: I have paid for my folly, shut away the heady young wine that intoxicated me, and folded up my big, floating heart, emptied of its three or four marvels. How well it has fought and striven! There, there, heart, gently now, let us take a rest. You despised happiness, we can do ourselves that justice. Cassandra, to whom I'm returning and who did not dare foretell everything, did tell us this: that we were in no danger of dying for love nor, God be praised, of thinking ourselves content with a modest little happiness.

Now that I'm far away from that period of my life when I inclined only in one direction, like those allegorical figures at the source of rivers, cradled and drawn along by their watery tresses, I can let it diminish. It is true that I gave myself without stinting, or at least I thought so. If one poses as a classical Goddess of Plenty, whose job is to empty her cornucopia no matter where, one risks the critical stare of the public circling round the pedestal and appraising the statue according to its weight of over-handsome womanhood: "Hmm . . . Doesn't one get a bit thinner when one gives out so much? How's this one managed to put on so much flesh?" People like you to waste away as a result of giving and they are quite right. The pelican is not expected to grow fat, the only way the ageing mistress can prove her selflessness is by letting a noble consumption make her pale, thereby leaving the field to a youthful cheek whipped with pink, and a ruddy lip. This rarely happens. On the contrary, to be perverse enough to gratify an adolescent lover up to the hilt doesn't ravage a woman sufficiently. Giving becomes a sort of neurosis, a fierce egotistical frenzy. "Here's a new tie, a cup of hot milk, a shred of my own live flesh, a box of cigarettes, a conversation, a journey, a kiss, a word of advice, the shelter of my arms, an idea. Take! And don't dream of refusing unless you want me to burst. I can't give you less, so put up with it!"

When a mother is still young and a mistress mature, rivalry in giving can poison both feminine hearts and cause a snarling hatred, a war of vixens in which it isn't the mother's clamour that is the less savage and the less indiscreet. Poor over-loved sons! Preening under feminine glances, wantonly nuzzled by the female who carried you, favourites from the deep night of the womb, beautiful cherished young males, whatever you do you can't help betraying when you pass from one mother to another. You yourself, my very dear mother, whom I liked to think untouched by my ordinary crimes, even in your correspondence I find, conveyed in a handwriting that strove in vain to hide the irregular pounding of your heart, these words: *"Yes, like you I've found Madame X very changed and sad. I know there is no mystery in her private life; so we can bet that big son of hers has his first mistress."*

If all one had to do, in the hope of one day running dry, were to keep on giving of oneself in great gushes, we "over-forties" could hardly fail. I know some who would accept the challenge right away: "Agreed! First that hell, which I can't do without; just one demon and afterwards peace, emptiness, blessed total peace, penury. . . ." How many sincerely hope that old age may arrive like a vulture that detaches itself from the sky and drops, after soaring for long invisible? And what then is old age? I shall learn. But when it comes I shall no longer be able to understand it. You, my very dear elder, will have disappeared without teaching me what old age is, for you wrote to me: *"Don't worry so much about my alleged arteriosclerosis. I'm better, and the proof is that at seven o'clock this morning I did the washing in my stream. I was enraptured. What a pleasure it is to dabble in clear water! I sawed wood, too, and made six little bundles of firewood. And I'm doing my housework myself again, which means it's being properly done. And after all, I'm only seventy-six!"*

You wrote to me that same day, a year before you died, and the loops of your capital B's, T's and J's, which have a kind of proud cap on the back of their heads, are radiant with gaiety. How rich you were that morning in your little house! At the end of the garden leapt a little stream, so swift that it immediately carried away everything that might have sullied it. You were rich with yet another morning, with a new victory over illness, rich with one more task, with the jewels of light glittering in the running water, with one more truce between you and all your pains. You were soaping linen in the stream, sighing because you could not get over the death of your beloved, you went "twee-e-e-e!" at the chaffinches, you were thinking that you would tell me about your morning, oh, you hoarder of treasure! What I amass is not of the same quality, but whatever of it may endure comes from the parallel though inferior seam, mixed with clay. And I haven't taken too long to understand that an age comes for a woman when, instead of clinging to beautiful feet that are impatient to roam the world, expressing herself in soothing words, boring tears and burning, ever-shorter sighs —an age comes when the only thing that is left for her is to enrich her own self.

She hoards and reckons up everything, even to blows and scars—a scar being a mark which she did not carry at birth, an acquisition. When she sighs, "Oh, what a lot of sorrows He endowed me with!" she is, in spite of herself, weighing the value of the word—the value of the gifts. Little by little she stows them tranquilly away. But there are so many of them that in time she is forced, as her treasure increases, to stand back a little from it, like a painter from his work. She stands back, and returns, and stands back again, pushing some scandalous detail into place, bringing into the light of day a memory drowned in shadow. By some unhoped-for art she becomes—equitable. Is anyone imagining as he reads me, that I'm portraying myself? Have patience: this is merely my model.

When a man's glance is following certain household preparations, especially those for a meal, there is apt to be a look on his face that combines religious attention, boredom and fear. Like cats, men dread sweeping, and the lighted stove, and soapy water being pushed with a broom over the tiled floor.

In honour of a local saint, who according to tradition presides over merry-makings, Segonzac, Carco, Régis Gignoux and Thérèse Dorny were to leave their hillside and eat a southern luncheon here: salads, stuffed *rascasse* and aubergine fritters, an everyday meal which I usually enriched with a roast bird.

Vial, who lives in a thimble painted pink three hundred metres away, was not happy that morning because the portable stove we used for ironing, fitted up as a charcoal grill, was taking up a corner of the terrace. So he made himself as small as a sporting dog on a wedding day.

"Vial, don't you think they'll like my sauce with the little chickens? Four little chickens split in half, beaten with the flat of the chopper, salted, peppered, and anointed with pure oil brushed on with a sprig of *pebreda*? The little leaves of the *pebreda*, and the taste of it, cling to the grilled flesh. Look at them, don't they look good!"

Vial looked at them and so did I. Good indeed! A little rosy blood remained in the broken joints of the plucked and mutilated chickens, and you could see the shape of the wings, and the young scales covering the little legs that had only this morning enjoyed running and scratching. Why not cook a child, too? My tirade petered out and Vial said not a word. I sighed as I beat my sharp, unctuous sauce, but soon the aroma of the delicate flesh, dripping on to the charcoal, would give me a yawning hunger. I think I may soon give up eating the flesh of animals; but not to-day.

"Tie my apron for me, Vial. Thank you. Next year . . ."

"What are you going to do, next year?"

"I shall be a vegetarian. Dip the tip of your finger in my sauce. Well? That sauce on tender little chickens . . . All the same—not this year, I'm too hungry—all the same I shall be a vegetarian."

"Why?"

"It would take too long to explain. When one stops liking a certain kind of cannibalism, all the other kinds leave of their own accord, like fleas from a dead hedgehog. Pour me out some oil, gently. . . ."

He bent his bare body, polished by sun and salt. His skin caught the light, so that he was green round the loins and blue on the shoulders, according as he moved, like the dyers of Fez. When I said "Stop!" he cut short the thread of golden oil and straightened himself, and I laid my hand caressingly for a moment on his chest, as one does with a horse. He looked at my hand, which proclaims my age—in fact it looks several years older—but I did not withdraw it. It is a good little hand, burnt dark brown, and the skin is getting rather loose round the joints and on the back. It has nails cut short, a thumb that readily bends back like a scorpion's tail, scars and scratches, and I'm not ashamed of it, rather the reverse. It has two pretty nails—a present from my mother—and three not very beautiful—a souvenir of my father.

"You've bathed? You went for a good four hundred metres along the shore? Well then why, when we're only in July, do you look as though it were the end of the holidays, Vial?"

The slightest emotional upset disturbs Vial's regular, rather beautiful features. He hasn't a gay expression, but he never looks sad. I say he's handsome because here, after a month's stay, all the men are handsome as a result of the hot sun, the sea, and their going naked.

"What have you brought me from the market, Vial? You didn't mind, did you? Divine only just had time to run and get the chickens."

"Two melons, an almond tart, and peaches. There are no more early figs and the others won't be ripe till . . ."

"I know that better than you, I inspect them every day in my vineyard. You're a darling. How much do I owe you?"

He shrugged to show he didn't know, his beautifully muscled shoulders rising and falling like a bosom breathing.

"You've forgotten? Wait while I see how big the melons are. That tart is the sixteen-franc size, and you have two kilos of peaches. Fourteen and sixteen make thirty, thirty and fifteen, forty-five. I owe you between forty-five and fifty francs."

"Have you got on your bathing-suit under your apron? Haven't you had time for a bathe?"

"Of course I have."

He licked the top of my arm, quite simply.

"It's true."

"Oh, you know, that might be yesterday evening's salt. Let's rest a bit, we've lots of time, they'll all be late."

"All right. Isn't there something useful I can do?"

"Yes, get married."

"Oh! I'm thirty-five."

"That's what I mean. It'll make you younger. You aren't young enough. That comes with age, according to Labiche. Your little friend didn't come back from the market with you? You must have met her on the port?"

"Mademoiselle Clément is finishing a study at Le Lavandou."

"You don't like my calling her your little friend, I see?"

"No, I don't. It's an expression that might make people think she's my mistress, when she's not."

I laughed as I powdered the overhot embers in the ironing-stove. I hardly know the type to which this boy, who lives very quietly, belongs. He is of the same generation as Carco, Segonzac, Léopold Marchand and Pierre Benoit, Mac-Orlan, Cocteau and Dignimont— those whom I knew when they were, as I like to say, "quite little", before and during the war. Was it at that time, when the irregular ebb and flow of leave used to bring them to Paris, that I got into the habit of *tutoying* nearly all of them on the strength of their faces, some oddly fat and others as hollow as those of schoolboys grown too fast? No, it's simply because they are young, and if they greet me with hugs and big smacking kisses on the cheek, that's also because they are young. But if the most sensitive among them—those that I've named and those I don't name—call me "Madame" and, for fun, "my good master", that is because they are they and I am I.

The almost naked youth who poured the oil for me this morning took part in the war too. When it was over, just as he was going to become an upholsterer again, he jibbed. He was afraid, he said, of a father who had remained vigorous, grasping in his business, and arrogant. I've sometimes wanted to write a story about a family devoured, bones and all, by its parents. I'd use as my model, for instance, Mme Lhermier, who kept her daughter tied to her apron-strings, prevented every chance of marriage and turned the stupid, docile girl into a sort of withered twin of herself, who never left her day or night, and never complained. But one day I saw the look on Mlle Lhermier's face. . . . Hor-

ror! Horror! I should borrow a few characteristics from
Albert X, a passionate victim and disturbing shadow of
his mother; and from Fernand Z, a frail banker who
waits in vain for the death of his robust banker father.
There are plenty of them, I should only have to choose.
The trouble is that Mauriac has already done *Genitrix*.
But I mustn't waste too much pity on Vial the son,
whose Christian name is ... What at this early stage!

"Vial, what's your Christian name?"

"Hector."

In my astonishment, I stopped trimming the stalks
of the first dahlias of the season that I had cut for the
table.

"Hector? I had an idea you were called ... Valère."

"So I am, but I wanted to make sure you'd more or
less forgotten it."

... on Vial the son, who artfully makes the most of
his long commercial apprenticeship and uses visiting-
cards inscribed *"Vial, Decorator"*. He is no longer an
upholsterer. He has a modest little shop in Paris, half
fancy-bookshop, half knick-knacks, the kind you see
everywhere. And because he likes the company of
painters he has taken to liking their paintings.

Among all the scribblers who have no time for anything but writing, he gives himself the luxury of reading,
designing furniture and even criticising us. He tells
Carco that he ought never to have published anything but verse, and Segonzac that he is a mystic. The
great "Dédé" doesn't laugh, and answers politely:
"Scoundrrrel! Son of a bitch, there's something in that,
your head's better scrrrewed on than your backside!"
Carco calls me to witness: "If a professional writer said
that to me, Colette, I'd call him a fat-head. But what on
earth can I say to an upholsterer? Mr Interior-decora-
tor, you come on too strong!"

I don't know much more about my oil-pourer. But
what do I know of my other friends? What we're doing,
first and foremost, when we seek friendship or give it
is to cry: "Sanctuary! Sanctuary!" That cry is certainly

the best thing in us, so we may as well keep the rest dark as long as possible.

I think that the presence of human beings in any number tires plants. Horticultural exhibits swoon and die almost every evening, when people have paid them too much attention; I found my garden weary after the departure of my friends. Perhaps flowers are sensitive to the sound of voices. And my flowers are no more accustomed to receptions than I am.

My guests gone, the cats creep out of their lairs, yawn, stretch as they do when they come out of their travelling baskets, and sniff the traces of the intruders. The sleepy tom-cat glides down from the mulberry tree like a liana. His ravishing companion, on the terrace which is given over to her again, displays her belly where there appears, in a cloud of bluish fur, a single rosy teat, for this season she has suckled only one kitten. The departure of the visitors in no way changes the habits of the Brabançon bitch who watches over me, doesn't stop and never has stopped watching over me, and will only at death cease to give me her whole attention. Her death alone can put an end to the drama of her life: to live with me or without me. She too is ageing sturdily.

Grouped round these three specimens of the ruling caste of animals, the second-rate creatures keep the place assigned them by a protocol not so much human as animal: the scrawny she-cats from the neighbouring farms, my caretaker's dogs transformed by a bath of white dust. "In summer here all the dogs belong to the eighteenth century," says Vial.

The swallows were already drinking in the wash-house and snapping up the mayflies when my "company" took itself off. The air had its stale afternoon flavour and it was very hot in the sun, which sets late. But it cannot deceive me, I decline with the day. And towards the end of each day the cat, winding herself about my ankles in a figure of eight, invites me to celebrate the approach of night. She is the third cat in my life, if I count only the cats of real character, memorable among both cats and she-cats.

Shall I ever marvel enough at animals? This one is exceptional, like a friend one will never replace, or a perfect lover. What is the source of the love she bears me? Of her own accord she adapted her pace to mine, and the invisible bond that links her to me gave me the idea of a collar and a leash. She got both and she wore them as though she were sighing: "At last!" Her narrow little lean face, rain-blue with eyes of pure gold, looks older and seems to get paler when the slightest thing worries her. She has the modesty that belongs to perfect lovers, and their dread of too-insistent contacts. I shall not say much more about her. All the rest is silence, faithfulness, impacts of soul, the shadow of an azure shape on the blue paper that receives everything I write, the silent passage of paws silvered with moisture.

After her, but a long way after, I have the tom-cat, her magnificent husband, all slumbrous with beauty and power, and as timid as a professional strong man. Then come all the creatures that fly, crawl and creak, the hedgehog of the vines, the innumerable lizards that the grass-snakes eat, the nocturnal toad which, when I gather it into the palm of my hand and hold it up towards the lantern, lets two crystal cries fall into the grass. The crab under the seaweed too, and the blue gurnard with martlet's wings that rises in flight from the waves. If it falls on the sand I pick it up stunned, encrusted with grit, and then put it back in the water and swim beside it, supporting its head. But I no longer like describing the appearance or writing stories of animals. The passage of the centuries never bridges the chasm which yawns between them and man. I shall end by hiding my own creatures except from a few friends, whom they shall choose. I shall show the cats to Philippe Berthelot, himself full of feline power, and to Vial, who is in love with the she-cat and pretends, as does Alfred Savoir, that I can conjure up a cat in a place where no cat exists. One doesn't love beasts and men at the same time. I am becoming daily more suspect to my fellows. But if they were my fellows I should not be suspect to them.

"When I enter a room where you're alone with your animals," my second husband used to say, "I feel I'm being indiscreet. One of these days you'll retire to a jungle." I keep toying with the agreeable picture of the future this prophecy offers me, though I've no wish to try and fathom what insidious—or impatient—suggestion may have lain behind it; but I dwell on it to remind myself of the deep, logical mistrust which it reveals in a very civilised man. I dwell on it as on a sentence written by the finger of a man on a forehead which, if one pushes aside the foliage of hair that covers it, probably smells, to a human sense of smell, of a lair, the blood of a hare, the belly of a squirrel, a bitch's milk. Any man who remains on the side of men has reason to shrink from a creature who opts for beasts and who smiles, strong in her dreadful innocence. "Your monstrous simplicity. . . . Your sweetness full of dark places. . . ." How true all those phrases were! From the human point of view monstrosity begins where there arises connivance with animals. Did not Marcel Schwob dub "sadistic monsters" those withered old bird-charmers one used to see in the Tuileries covered with birds? Connivance alone would be one thing but there is preference too, and at this point I shall keep silent. I stop short also when it comes to arenas and menageries. For if I see no objection to putting into the hands of the public, in print, rearranged fragments of my emotional life, it's understandable that I should tie up tight in the same sack, strictly private, all that concerns a *preference* for animals and—it's a question of partiality too—the child whom I brought into the world. How charming she is, that child, when she scratches, in a thoughtful, friendly way, the granular head of a huge toad. . . . Ssh! Once upon a time I took upon myself to make a girl of fourteen or fifteen the heroine of a novel. May I be forgiven, for I did not then know what I was doing.

"You'll retire to a jungle. . . ." So be it. And I mustn't wait too long. I mustn't wait until I notice the first waverings in the graph of my relation and exchanges with animals. The wish to captivate, in other words to dominate, the different ways of wrapping up a wish or an order and directing them to their end, these I feel are still flexible in me—but for how long?

A poor lioness, a beautiful creature, recently picked me out from the bunch of gapers massed before her bars. Having chosen me she came out of her long despair as out of a sleep, and not knowing how to show that she had recognised me, that she wanted to confront me, to question me, perhaps to love me to the point where she could accept only me as a victim, she threatened, sparked and roared like a captive fire, hurled herself against the bars and then suddenly, wearied, grew drowsy, still looking at me.

The mental hearing, that I can project towards the Beast, still functions. The tragedies of birds in the air, the subterranean combats of rodents, the suddenly increased sound of a swarm on the warpath, the hopeless look of horses and donkeys are so many messages addressed to me. I no longer want to marry anyone, but I still dream that I am marrying a very big cat. No doubt Montherlant would be delighted to learn it.

Love and respect for living creatures could be read in my mother's letters and in her heart. So I know where the spring of my vocation lay, a spring which I muddied as soon as I was born through my passion for touching and stirring up the depths lying beneath the pure stream. I accuse myself of having from an early age, not content with loving them, wanted to shine in the eyes of these, my kin and my accomplices. It is an ambition I still have.

"So you don't like fame?" Madame de Noailles asked me.

But I do. I would like to leave a great reputation

among those creatures who having kept, on their fur
and in their souls, the trace of my passage, madly
hoped for a single moment that I belonged to them.

My team of young guests was very attractive this
morning. Two had brought with them young women
who were extremely pretty, and so well behaved that
you might think each of them had been told: "I'm
going to take you to Colette's, you know, but I must
remind you that she doesn't like bird-like cries or
literary views. Put on your prettiest frock, the pink
one, or the blue. You'll pour out the coffee." They
know that the young women I find agreeable are pretty
and rather reserved. They are well aware of the things
that charm my leisure hours: children, ceremonious
young women, and saucy animals.

Some painters have wives or mistresses who are
worthy of them and of the life they lead. They look
gentle and have the same sort of habits as farmers'
wives. For don't the men get up at daybreak and go
off to the fields or the forest or along the shore? And
don't they return at nightfall, tired and silent with
solitude? While they are away the women cut out
summer frocks from tablecloths, or make napkins and
serviettes out of cotton handkerchiefs, and go to market
without affectation, that is to say to buy provisions and
not to exclaim at the "beautiful consistency" of the
red-lacquered *rascasses* or the bellies of the *girelles,*
striped ochre and azure.

"My man? He must be in the fields, over there
towards Pampelonne," answers the mistress of Luc-
Albert Moreau, pointing to the horizon with the vague
gesture of a peasant woman. Asselin sings like a cow-
herd and sometimes, if you strain your ear, the breeze
brings you the sweet voice of Dignimont, chanting a
little soldier's or sailor's lament.

Hélène Clément, who came alone, was by no means
the plainest. She doesn't belong in the camp of the

models, nor in that of the women who are submissive to men. She is a straw blonde, with straight hair. The sun tans her a harmonious red, a beautiful even red that floods her blonde skin and pledges her grey eyes to remain blue all summer. Tall, and slenderly built, almost her only fault is that she is too straightforward physically and morally, which is one of the snobberies that you find in girls of twenty-five. It is fair to say that I don't know her very well.

She paints in an obstinate way, with big virile strokes, swims, drives her five-horse-power car, and often goes to see her parents, who spend the summer in the mountains because they dread the heat. She lives in a *pension de famille* so that everyone knows that she is a "serious-minded girl". Thirty years ago one met Hélène Clément at seaside places, a piece of embroidery in her hand. Nowadays she paints the sea and rubs herself with coconut oil. She has the same pretty, docile countenance as the Hélène Cléments of other days, the same bodily dignity and above all the deferential way of answering: "Yes, Madame. Thank you, Madame" which, cropping up in the middle of the language she has learnt from the painters and the wild young men, half opens the garden gate of the boarding school again. What I like in this big creature is precisely that air of having let fall her old embroidery, that embroidery which in her took the place of mystery. I may be mistaken, because I do not pay enough attention to Hélène. Perhaps too the transparency of body and soul which she seems to prize so much lets me guess too easily the presence of that sad irresolution which—though they deny it—is characteristic of those so-called independent women who do no wrong—if one is still, as in former days, to call carnal intercourse "wrong".

No one else will come. I shan't leave this table for the little café at the port where people gather to watch the flamboyant sunsets. Towards the end of the day the sun gathers together the scraps of cloud evaporated by the warm sea, draws them to the sky's rim and twists

them into rags of fire, then stretches them out into
ruddy bands and, as it touches *Les Maures,* burns itself
out. But this month it sets too late. I shall admire it
well enough as I dine alone, my back against the wall
of my terrace. I've had my fill of pleasant faces to-day.
So instead the bitch, the she-cat and I will walk towards
that great spread of violet that rises from the sea and
shows where the East lies. Soon it will be the hour
when some old people return home, neighbours of mine
who work in the fields. I can only bear old people when
they are bent earthwards, chapped and chalky, with
hands like wood and hair like a bird's nest. Some of
them offer me, in the hollow of a palm drained of human moisture and colour, the most precious thing they
have managed to procure: an egg, a chicken, a round
apple, a rose, a grape. A Provençal woman of seventy-
two goes every day from the port to her field of vines
and vegetables, two kilometres in the morning and the
same in the evening. No doubt she will die of toil, but
she doesn't seem tired when she sits down for a moment before my gate. She gives light cries: "My! How
pretty it is!" I hurry there: with a carved, blackened,
hooked finger she is stroking the flat-headed bud, like
a snake ready to hiss, of one of those sea-shore lilies
that shoot out of the earth, grow so quickly that one
dare not look at them, spread forth their corollas and
their maleficent odour like that of a ripe, bruised fruit,
and then return to nothingness.

No, it was not pretty. It looked like a strong, blind
young serpent. But the old woman knew that it would
be pretty a few days later. She had had time to learn
that. There were moments when, seeing her laden with
green peppers, a necklace of new onions round her
neck, her hands of dried osier half-closed on an egg she
never lets fall, I could love her if I didn't suddenly rec-
ollect that, though she no longer has the strength to
create, she keeps the strength to destroy, and that she
crushes the shrew-mouse on the path, the dragonfly
against the window-pane, and the still-moist new-born

kitten. She makes no distinction between that and shelling peas. So that is why, when I pass her, I say "Goodbye!" and let her fade into the landscape, her and her shadow, a tiny old man who lives like a lizard in a stone hut under an oleander. The old woman talks, the old man no longer does. He has nothing left to say to anyone. No longer able to dig, he scratches the earth, and when he sweeps the threshold of his hut he looks as if he were playing because he uses a child's broom. The other day they found an old person dead and quite dry, like a dead toad burnt up by the mid-day heat before a bird of prey had had time to gut it. Death becomes more decent to our living eyes when it is thus cheated of much of its corruption. Will my own final lot be that of a light friable body, hollow bones and a great devouring sun over it all? Sometimes I force myself to think of it so as to persuade myself that the second half of my life is making me take a little more thought and care for what happens *after*. . . . The illusion soon passes. Death does not interest me—not even my own.

We have dined well. We have walked on the coast road, along its most populated part, the narrow flowery marsh where hemp agrimony, statice and scabious contribute three shades of mauve, the tall flowering reed its cluster of brown edible seeds, the myrtle its white scent—white, white and bitter, pricking the tonsils, white to the point of causing nausea and ecstasy—the tamarisk its rosy mist and the bulrush its beaver-furred club. This place teems with life, especially at daybreak and when the birds are going to bed. The reed warbler slides endlessly, for fun, down the stems of the reeds and each time shouts for joy. The swallows skim the sea, the tits, drunk with courage, expel from this paradise the troops of jays, thirsty wasps and poaching cats; and in the middle of the day, heavy Camberwell Beauties, trailing the thick velvet of their wings, yellow

Flambés, striped like tigers, and swallow-tails with gothic veining flutter over the sickly-sweet little lagoon, salted by the sea and sweetened by roots and grasses, and come to pump the honey from the pink agrimony, the bird's-foot trefoil and the mints, each butterfly voluptuously attached to its flower.

In the evening animal life hides a little but barely diminishes. What secret laughter there is, what swift leapings under my footsteps, what lightning flights before the spring of the two cats who have followed me! For in their night livery they are redoubtable. The gentle she-cat shoots through the bushes with a single bound while her powerful male, once aroused, scatters the stones of the road like a horse as he gallops along, and both of them, without hunger, crunch the glowing-eyed hawkmoths.

The cool of the evening here brings for me a shiver that resembles a laugh, a cloak of fresh air on my bare flesh, and a feeling of pity which tightens its grip on me as night closes in. If I had any confidence in that moment of gentleness, then would be the time for me to grow in stature, to adopt a brave attitude, to dare and die. But every time I avoid it. To grow. . . . For whom? To dare. . . . What more could I dare, then? I've been told often enough that to live first as love dictates, and then as the absence of love dictates, shows the most overweening conceit. It's so good to be flush with the earth, to become once more a prey to plants just tall enough to provide shade for my forehead, paws which reach up to seek my hand, furrows asking for water, a tender letter that wants an answer, a red lamp in the green of the night, a notebook of smooth paper that I must embroider with my writing —I am back again, as I am every evening. How near the dawn is! This month night gives herself to the earth as to a secret lover, quickly and a little at a time. It is ten o'clock. In four hours it will no longer be real night. Besides, a great round mouth of a moon, rather frightening, is invading the sky, and she is no friend of mine.

Three hundred metres away Vial's lamp, in his thimble-shaped house, looks at mine. Whatever can the boy be up to, instead of shuffling in his *espadrilles* along to the little port, or dancing—he dances so well —at the little dance-hall on the jetty? He's too quiet. One of these days I must give my mind to the question seriously, and marry him to that other sober creature, Hélène Clément—oh, only for as long as they want. I noticed to-day a shade of difference in her, in her expression that's to say, when she spoke to him. She was laughing with all the others, especially when Carco, his eyelids half-closed like a hunter's over his caramel-coloured eyes, revealed to her the shocking and prodigious secret of an old prostitute who managed to retain her childish innocence for twenty-five years in the Latin Quarter. Hélène isn't prudish about what she hears, far from it. But her laugh, at Carco's stories, is for all that the laugh of that long-ago Hélène Clément who dropped her embroidery frame when her cousin the polytechnician—"Oh, Henry, will you be quiet!"— told her, as he pushed the swing, that he had caught a glimpse of her ankle. Hélène Clément reserves for Vial that side of her that is closest to truth: the serious face of a girl who only wants to be simple. It isn't possible that Vial should not have noticed it.

Normally I am not much given to making plans for two people to be happy together, but I have the feeling that I am responsible for that uncomfortable little agitation, that setting in motion of idle forces which might in future engulf two beings hitherto far apart, each safely sheltered in personal privacy, or lack of it.

When I was driving my little car to market yesterday morning, about nine o'clock, I passed and then picked up Hélène Clément who, her bare head glossy as a golden apple, was on her way, with a canvas under her arm, to the carpenter who acts as frame-maker. Two hundred metres further on, behind his gate and on the threshold of the "Thimble", Vial was scraping an antique armchair, as dry, convoluted and delicate as a hawthorn in winter.

"Vial, we haven't seen you for two days! What's that armchair, Vial?"

His laugh was a white bar in his dark face.

"You're not going to have this one! I went further than Moustier-Sainte-Marie to get it, with the Citroën."

"So that was it," said Hélène.

Vial raised his head, his smile fading.

"What d'you mean, that was it?"

She said nothing and gave him so dangerously stupid a look that he could have read what he liked in those grey eyes, wide open in the sun. I jumped out of the car.

"Show us, Vial, do show us! And treat us to a morning glass of white wine and cold water!"

Hélène got out after me and sniffed the smell of the unfamiliar little dwelling, furnished with a divan and a half-moon-shaped ship's table and brightened with pink linen hangings and white Moustier pottery.

"A Juan Gris, two Dignimonts, a colour print by Linder," counted Hélène. "That's Vial all over, always chopping and changing. You think that's the right thing for the walls of a house down here?"

Vial, who was wiping his stained hands, looked at Hélène. She was leaning with one hand against the wall, neck and arms braced as if for a climb, and her bare feet in sandals as she stood on tiptoe were far from ugly. And how beautiful that red earthenware colour of her whole body, so lightly clad!

"Vial, how much did you pay for your armchair?"

"A hundred and ninety francs. And it's walnut, under the paint that some brute has covered it with. Look at the arm I've scraped. . . ."

"Vial, sell it to me!"

He shook his head.

"Vial, are you a dealer or aren't you? Vial, have you no heart?"

He shook his head.

"Vial, I'll swop your armchair for . . . for Hélène, there now!"

"Is she yours then?"

For wit and delicacy there was nothing to choose between my jest and his reply.

"That's settled then!" bantered Hélène. "Really, my dear, you've got a bargain!"

She laughed, redder than her red sunburn, and in each of her grey blue eyes danced a glittering speck of light. But Vial once again shook his head and the two glittering specks changed to tears.

"Hélène!"

Already she was running away from the house and Vial and I looked after her.

"What's the matter with her?"

"I don't know," said Vial coldly.

"It's your fault."

"I didn't say anything."

"You went 'no, no' like this."

"And if I'd gone 'yes, yes' like this, would it have been better?"

"You bore me, Vial, I'm going. I'll tell you to-morrow how it turns out."

"Oh, you know . . ."

He shrugged a shoulder, let it fall, and walked with me to the garden gate.

In my little car a dry-eyed Hélène was humming as she gazed at the freshly-painted picture balanced on her knees.

"D'you see anything in this, Madame Colette?"

I found a few words to say as I looked at the straightforward study, which she had unnecessarily overpainted in order to be "a real painter", and then, forgetting prudence, I added, "Did Vial hurt you? I do hope not."

She answered me with a coldness that seemed to me exactly like Vial's. "I beg of you, Madame Colette, don't confuse humiliation with pain. Yes, yes, humilia-

tion. Accidents like that often happen to me in this particular milieu."

"What milieu?"

Hélène made a slight movement of the shoulders,
compressed her lips, and I felt she was displeased with
herself. Then she turned to me with a sudden burst of
honesty which made my little car skid on that poetic
road that is never repaired.

"Madame Colette, don't take what I say amiss. I say
'this milieu' because after all it isn't the milieu in which
I was brought up. I say 'this milieu' because although
I like it very much I sometimes feel an outsider among
the painters and their girl-friends. But all the same I'm
intelligent enough to . . ."

". . . to understand life."

She protested with her whole body.

"I beg you, Madame Colette, don't treat me—you
sometimes do!—like a little bourgeoise who's playing
at being a 'Montparno' type. I do indeed understand
quite a few things, and above all that Vial, who doesn't
belong to 'this milieu' either, doesn't go down well
when he jokes in a certain way and permits himself
certain liberties. He puts neither grace nor gaiety into
it, and what would be charming and jolly on the lips of
either Dédé or Kiss, for instance, sounds shocking on
his."

"But he didn't say anything," I put in as I pulled up
in front of the "First Class Pension" where Hélène
stays.

Standing by the little car and holding out her hand,
my young passenger could not conceal her irritation, or
the glitter in her eyes, moist once again, in which was
reflected the triumphant blue all about us.

"If you don't mind, Madame Colette, let's say no
more about it. I have no wish to let this story, which
isn't one, drag on for ever, even for the pleasure of
listening to the defence of Vial, above all presented by
you! . . . Presented by you!"

She fled, rather too big for such childish misery. I

called after her: "Goodbye! Goodbye!" in a kind way, so that our brusque separation should not awaken the curiosity of the sculptor, Lejeune, who at that moment was crossing the little square. He was dressed, in all innocence, in *eau de Nil* cotton shorts with a sleeveless pink jacket, open over a sweater embroidered with little flowers in cross-stitch, and he greeted us by raising a wide-brimmed rush hat trimmed with woollen cherries.

It was because of that silly Hélène that I bore with Vial's presence absentmindedly on the following afternoon, and enjoyed it less than usual. Yet he had brought me some bars of nougat, and branches of a carob tree with green fruit, which keep fresh a long time if one sticks them in earthenware jars full of moist sand.

After the five o'clock bathe he was sprawling indolently on the terrace, as he did every day. It had been a wind-whipped bathe, and so cold under a fierce sun—for the Mediterranean is full of surprises—that instead of the shelter of the pink room we sought the warm, living, beaten earth under the checkered shade of wide-spaced branches. Five o'clock in the afternoon is a wavering golden hour which momentarily ruffles the universal blue of air and water in which we bathe. The wind had not yet risen but a ripple was noticeable among the featheriest foliage, that of the mimosa, for instance, and a faint signal waved by one branch of a pine was answered by another pine branch, which nodded all by itef.

"Vial, don't you think it's less blue than yesterday?"

"What is less blue?" murmured Vial, bronze in his white slip.

He was lying nearly flat, his forehead on his folded arms; I always like him better when he hides his face. Not that he is ugly, but the lines of his face look rather sleepy above his clear-cut, alert, expressive body. I haven't omitted to point out to Vial that he might be guillotined without anyone's noticing.

"Everything is less blue. Or else it may be me. Blueness is mental. Blue doesn't make you hungry, or voluptuous. A blue room is uninhabitable. . . ."

"Since when?"

"Since I've said so! Unless you no longer hope for anything—in which case you can live in a blue room."

"Why me?"

"By you I mean anybody."

"Thank you. Why have you got blood on your leg?"

"It's my own. I stumbled against that commonest of shore plants, the broken bottle."

"Why is your left ankle always a little swollen?"

"And what about you, why were you caddish to the little Clément girl, come to that?"

The bronze man sat up, with an air of dignity.

"I wasn't caddish to the . . . to Mademoiselle Clément. But if what you have in mind is a marriage, I shall be infinitely obliged to you, Madame, if you'll stop talking to me about her!"

"How romantic you are, Vial! Mayn't we have a little laugh? Move along, you're taking up all the room on this parapet, and let me tell you, you don't know everything. When she left me yesterday she forbade me to undertake your defence. And she swept off like a tragedy queen repeating 'Above all not you! Above all not you!' Would you believe it?"

Vial leapt to his feet and planted himself before me, black as a baker's boy from hell.

"She said that to you? She dared?"

He faced me with a look so wide-eyed, so comically unlike himself, that I couldn't keep a straight face—I laugh more easily than I used to. The look of respectability which Vial's frequent silences, his habit of looking down and a certain sureness in his attitude give him, disintegrated completely and I did not find him pretty. He pulled himself together with a pleasing promptness and sighed casually, "Poor little thing!"

"You're sorry for her?"

"What about you?"

"Vial, I don't much like your habit of always answering a question by another question. It's not polite. As far as I'm concerned, you realise, I can hardly be said to know the girl. . . ."

"Neither do I."

"Oh! I thought . . . But she isn't difficult to know. She gives the impression of shunning mystery as though it were a microbe. Hullo! Coo-ee! Isn't that Géraldy, coming back from Les Salins?"

"Yes, I think it is."

"Why didn't he stop?"

"He didn't hear you, the noise of his gears drown all other sounds."

"But he did, he looked round. It's you who frightened him. I was saying to you that little Hélène Clément . . ."

"Will you excuse me? I want to go and get my sweater. People from the north call Provence a hot country. . . ."

Vial took himself off and I became more aware of the warmth, the freshness, the increased slant of the light, the universal blue, a few sails on the sea, and the near-by fig tree spreading its odour of milk and flowering grass. A tiny little tuft of fire was smoking on a mountain. The sky turned pink where it touched the harsh azure of a Mediterranean, as ripply as an animal's coat, and the she-cat for no apparent reason began to smile at me. The thing is that she loves solitude, by which I mean my presence, and her smile made me realise that for the first time I was treating Vial as a third party of importance.

His absence left me with a sense of emptiness and airy well-being; did that mean that his presence was enough to fill up the former and prevent the latter? At the same moment I understood that the reason why Géraldy had not interrupted the noise of his tortured engine in front of my door was because Vial, visible from the road, was with me; and that if my friends and

companions had all quietly given up coming round
about five o'clock to my crescent-shaped bay where the
sand, under the weight of blue water, is so firm and
white, it was because they felt sure that they would
meet there, in addition to myself, the half-silent, vague-
ly-bored Valère Vial, keeping his distance, running
with the hare but hunting with the hounds.

That's all it is, a slight misunderstanding. I've
thought it well over, not for long, since there's no point
in thinking for long at a time and there's nothing in this
particular matter that merits it. I can't believe that this
young man is in any way calculating. It is true that,
though I've often been taken in, I've not learnt to be
suspicious. What I would rather fear, for him, is some
form of amorous attachment. I write that without
laughing, and, raising my head, I look at myself, without laughing, in the inclined mirror; then I turn to my
writing again.

No other fear, not even that of ridicule, prevents me
from writing these lines which I am willing to risk will
be published. Why should I stop my hand from gliding
over this paper to which for so many years I've con-
fided what I know about myself, what I've tried to hide,
what I've invented and what I've guessed? At no time
has the catastrophe of love, in all its phases and con-
sequences, formed a part of the true intimate life of a
woman. Why do men—writers or so-called writers—
still show surprise that a woman should so easily reveal
to the public love-secrets and amorous lies and half-
truths? By divulging these, she manages to hide other
important and obscure secrets which she herself does
not understand very well. The spotlight, the shameless
eye which she obligingly operates, always explores the
same sector of a woman's life, that sector tortured by
bliss and discord round which the shades are thickest.
But it is not in the illuminated zone that the darkest
plots are woven. Man, my friend, you willingly make
fun of women's writings because they can't help being

autobiographical. On whom then were you relying to
paint women for you, din them into your ears, debase
them in your eyes, in short make you tired of them?
On yourself? You have become my friend too recently
for me to give you my opinion on that. We were saying, then, that Vial . . .

How beautiful the night is, once again! How good
it is, in the depths of such a night, to contemplate
seriously something that is no longer serious! Seriously,
for it is no laughing matter. This is not the first time
that a veiled, unfamiliar ardour has tried first to restrict
and then to break the circle within which I live so
trustingly. These involuntary conquests have nothing to
do with a time of life. We must look for their origin in
literature—and this is where my responsibility begins.
I write this humbly and conscientiously. When readers
take to writing to an author, especially to a woman
author, they don't easily lose the habit. Vial, who has
only known me for two or three summers, must still be
trying to find me in two or three of my novels—if I dare
call them novels. There are still young girls—too young
to notice the dates of editions—who write to tell me
they have read the *Claudine* books in secret and that
they will look for my answer at the *poste restante* . . .
if indeed they do not give me an assignation in a tea-
shop. Perhaps they see me in a school-girl's uniform—
who knows, in socks? Not long before his death Catulle
Mendès said to me: "You won't be able to gauge until
much later the power of the literary type you've
created." Why did I not ignore all masculine sugges-
tions and create a type which by its simplicity and
even by its resemblance would have been more worthy
to endure? But let us go back to Vial and Hélène
Clément. . . .

A worn old moon is wandering along the horizon
pursued by a surprisingly neat and metallic-looking
little cloud, grabbing at the bitten disk as a fish grabs a
floating slice of fruit. There is still no promise of rain

there. We want rain for the gardens and the orchards. The unfathomable blue of the night, powdered with stars, makes my rather bare pink walls look pinker still when I turn and look at them. An oriental coolness clings to the walls, and the sparse pieces of furniture breathe at their ease. Only in this sun-steeped country can a heavy table, a wicker chair, an earthenware jar crowned with flowers, and a dish whose thick enamelling has run over the edge, make a complete furnishing. Segonzac decorates his "hall", vast as a barn, with rustic trophies only: crossed scythes and rakes, two-pronged forks of polished wood, wreaths of wheat-ears and red-handled whips, whose plaited tresses add a flourish to the wall. In the same way in Vial's "Thimble" . . .

Yes, let's get back to Vial. I am capering round Vial to-night in the way that a filly plays up before the start and then, after countless frolicsome curvettings, gently faces the tapes. I am not afraid of being emotionally stirred; but I am afraid of being bored. I am afraid of the appetite for drama and solemnity that young people have—especially Hélène Clément. How pleasant Vial was yesterday! Already he's less so. I compare his look to-day with that of yesterday. In spite of myself I see a meaning in his good-neighbourly faithfulness, in his long silences and in his favourite attitude, his head resting on his folded arms. I try to interpret his outbursts of questioning, evoking the sound of them: "Is it true that . . . who could have given you the idea of such a character? Didn't you know So-and-so, about the time when you were writing such-and-such a book? . . . I say, if I'm being indiscreet, send me packing. . . ." And then this evening, to crown all, when he repeated: "She dared! She dared!" with all the histrionics of a juvenile lead.

So here—at a time of life when I accept only the flower of any pleasure and the best of whatever is best, since I no longer demand anything—here is a fruit out of season, ripened by my easy familiarity: "Hi, young man, stand me a dozen Portuguese oysters, here without sitting down, Marseilles fashion. To-morrow we'll get up at six, Vial, and go and buy roses at the Halles, them's my orders!"—and also by my reputation, which is open to various interpretations.

And what if I were to be less gentle, to myself and others, from now until the end of this beautiful Provençal season starred with gleaming geraniums, white frocks, and half-opened water-melons showing their hearts glowing like planets! Yet nothing was threatening my happy summer of blue salt and crystal, my summer of open windows and swinging doors, my summer of necklaces of young garlic white as jasmine.

The amorous attachment of Vial and the no less amorous resentment of the little Clément girl—however little I like it I am placed between those two streams of emotion. I'm trying to understand them and quickly jotting down my comments. No matter if I incur ridicule—but it's true, there is the ridiculous side of it. It is hardly worth my remembering it, since in a moment I shall have forgotten it. It wasn't from you, my very dear mother—where are you watching, at this hour of your daily watch?—that I could have learnt this hesitation at the moment for helping, with hand and shoulder, an exhausted cart-horse, of gathering up a muddy dog in the fold of a skirt, of persuading and sheltering a shivering hostile child that was none of ours, or of shouldering impartially the weight of a stammering love in danger of falling into more mortal abysses. If I insert into our common liability some disorder that you don't recognise, forgive me. *"At my age there is only one virtue left: not to hurt anyone."* It was you who said that. I haven't, my very dear, your light step for treading certain paths. I remember how, on rainy days, you hardly ever had mud on your shoes. And I still see your light foot making a detour to spare a little grass-snake, stretched out happily on a warm path. I haven't got the blind certainty with which you blissfully examined both "good" and "evil", nor your art of giving new names, according to your code, to embittered old virtues and poor sins that have been waiting for centuries for their share of paradise. What you shunned in virtue was its pestilential austerity. How I love that letter of yours: *"The tea was given in honour of some very ugly women. Were we celebrating their ugliness? They bring their sewing and they work and work with an application that gives me the creeps. Why does it always seem to me that they are doing something evil?"* Sickened, you sensed a kindliness that could easily have committed more than one crime.

Here is the dawn. To-day it is all little clouds like a shower of petals, a dawn for those with hearts at rest. Raising myself by my wrists I can perceive, already emerging from the shadow pursued by the light, a swallow-dark sea and the "Thimble", still with no real colour, the "Thimble" where lies a solitary young man, ripening one secret too many. Solitary . . . it's a beauti-ful-looking word, beginning with its capital S rearing like a protective serpent. I can't entirely isolate it from the fierce glitter it receives from the solitaire diamond, the fierce glitter of Vial. Poor fellow! Now why didn't I think of exclaiming "Poor Hélène Clément!"? I'm fond of catching myself red-handed. In Morocco I called on some owners of great farms, voluntary exiles from France, entirely devoted to their vast Moroccan lands. They had retained a strange practice, in reading the papers, of pouncing on the word "Paris" with the ap-petite and smiles of people at a feast. For me, O Man, you are the fatherland; is that why you remain the first of my cares? I see no reason why not. But now, you cares, you little summer love-affairs, you must die here as the shadow round my lamp is dying; the arrogant song of a blackbird comes rolling up to me like big round pearls dropping from a broken thread. The night-scented fragrance of the pines will soon dissolve in the rising sun. This is the perfect hour for going to search, in the half-awakened sea where each movement of my bare legs breaks an iridescent film of pink enamel on the heavy blue of the water, for that quilt of seaweed that I need to protect the foot of the young tangerine trees.

Minet-Chéri,

It's not quite five in the morning. I'm writing to you by the light of my lamp and that of a fire just across the way, it's Mme Moreau's barn burning. Has someone set fire to it on purpose? It's full of fodder. The firemen are down there in my little garden. They're trampling on the borders I've prepared for flowers and strawberry plants. It's raining fire on my hen-house; what luck that I'd decided to rear no more chickens! It used to give me the horrors to eat, or make others eat, trusting hens that I had fed myself. How beautiful this fire is! I wonder if you've inherited my love of disasters? Oh dear, there go the poor rats that have escaped from the burning barn, squeaking and running in all directions. I expect they'll take refuge in my woodshed. Don't worry about anything else, by good fortune the wind is in the East. You realise that, if it were in the West, I should be roasted already. As I myself can be of no help, and since it's nothing but straw. I can give myself over to my love of tempests, the noise of the wind, and flames in the open air. . . . Now that I've reassured you by writing, I shall go and drink my morning coffee, and gaze at the beautiful fire."

"Naturally I don't dare offer you such a small thing," repeated Hélène Clément for the second time.

The small thing, which she had brought me yesterday, was a seascape, seen between prickly pears zinc blue against the chemical blue of the sea, a very concentrated study, as always a little too solid.

"Yet you came to offer it to me, Hélène?"

"Yes . . . because it's blue and because you like to surround yourself with different blues. But one shouldn't dare offer you such small things, should one?"

Had she then seen "big things" in my house? With a sweeping gesture I was able to clear myself of such a charge. I thanked her and she graciously propped her canvas up on the edge of a shelf, just where a stiff little lightning-coloured sunbeam pierced the shadow between two shutters. The canvas gleamed with all its blues, showing up all its painter's tricks as a made-up face reveals its secrets under the blaze of a spot-light, and Hélène sighed.

"You see," she said, "it isn't good."

"What do you think is the matter with it?"

"That it's by me, that's all. By someone else it would be better. Painting's difficult."

"So is writing."

"Do you mean that?"

She put this banal question to me in an anxious tone of voice, full of incredulity and surprise.

"It certainly is."

In the half-light that I arrange and cherish, every afternoon, with as much care as I would a bouquet, the eyes of this young girl became dark green, and I admired, below her hair that was no longer blonde, the perfect, glowing, red earthenware of her neck, a sturdy and supple column; long, like those of people of limited intelligence, but at the same time thick, revealing strength, the desire to succeed, and self-confidence.

"You were working, Madame?"

"No, never at this hour, at least not in summer."

"So I'm disturbing you less than if I'd come at another time."

"If you were disturbing me I should send you away."

"Yes. Would you like me to make you some lemonade?"

"No, thank you—unless you're thirsty? Forgive me, I'm being a very poor hostess."

"Oh!"

She made a vague gesture with her hand, picked up a book and opened it. The white page caught the gleam of bright light that clove the shadow and, like a mirror, reflected it upward on to the ceiling. For games of that kind the powerful summer light seizes the slightest object, brings it into the open and either glorifies it or dissolves it to nothing. The noonday sun turns the red geraniums black and casts vertically down on us a sad, ashen light. At noon the only pure azure in the landscape is that of the short shadows huddled close at the foot of walls and trees. I was waiting patiently for Hélène Clément to go. She merely raised her arm to smooth her hair with the flat of her hand. Even without seeing her I should have known from this gesture that she was blonde, healthily and rather pungently blonde; blonde and upset, on edge—there was no doubt of it. Embarrassed, she quickly lowered her bare arm, a beautiful ruddy handle, still rather flat between the shoulder and the elbow.

"You have very pretty arms, Hélène."

She smiled for the first time since she had come in, and paid me the compliment of looking confused. For if women and young girls quite calmly receive compliments from men on particular attractions in their bodies, a word of praise from a woman flatters them more and makes them glow with a mixture of embarrassment and pleasure that sometimes goes quite deep. Hélène smiled and then shrugged her shoulders.

"Where does that get me, with my luck?"

"Could it get you somewhere then, if it weren't for your luck?"

I was artfully using in this case that method of the interrogative answer that I found fault with in Vial.

She looked at me frankly, helped by the half-light which changed her into a brown-haired young woman with dark green eyes.

"Madame Colette," she began without much effort, "you've been kind enough to treat me, last summer and this, as . . . really as a . . ."

"Little chum?" I suggested.

"Two days ago, Madame, chum is just the word I should have used. I should probably have added that I was sick of it, and sick of all the pals, or something equally personal. To-day I can't think of any slang. I hardly ever do think of slang with you, Madame Colette."

"I can get along without it, Hélène."

The child was heating my cool room and her emotion thickened the air. At first my only grudge against her was for that, and for shortening my day. And besides, I knew Hélène's secret and I was afraid of being bored. Already in thought I was escaping to the burning, beaten earth of the terrace and listening to the crickets, which, revived by my noticing them, were sawing the dog-day into tiny splinters. With a start I became aware of all that was shining on the other side of the shutters, and hesitated no longer to show my impatience with a "Well, Hélène?" that a grown-up woman would have taken for a barely polite dismissal. But Hélène is every inch a young girl and she showed it very clearly. She threw herself on that "Well?" with the simplicity of an animal that has never yet known a snare, and spoke.

"Well, Madame, I want to show you that I'm worthy of confidence . . . in short, of the welcome you've given me. I don't want you to think me either a liar or . . . In short, Madame Colette, it's true that I live in a very independent way and that I work. But after all, you know life well enough to understand that there are times when things aren't easy, that I'm a woman like any other . . . that one can't avoid certain affections . . . certain hopes, and it's just in that particular hope that I've been disappointed, cruelly disappointed, for I had reason to believe . . . In this very place, last year, Madame, he spoke to me in unambiguous terms."

Less out of malice than to allow her to draw breath, I asked: "Who?"

She pronounced his name musically: "Vial, Madame."

The reproach that I read in her eyes blamed, not my curiosity, but certainly the artifice which she judged unworthy of us. So I protested.

"I know very well it's Vial, my dear. And what can we do about it?"

She fell silent, half-opened her mouth and then bit her parched lips. While we were speaking the stiff shaft of sunlight, spangled with dust, had reached far enough to burn her shoulder and, as though it were a fly, Hélène moved her arm and brushed the spot of light away with her hand. What she still had to say did not pass her lips. She still had to say to me, "Madame, I believe you are the . . . the friend of Vial, and that is why Vial cannot love me." I might easily have said it for her, but the moments passed and neither of us made up our mind to speak. Hélène pushed her armchair back a little and the blaze of light caressed her face. I felt sure that in an instant the whole of that youthful planet, with its bare, rounded, moon-like forehead and cheeks, was going to crack up, rent by an earthquake of sobs. The white down round her mouth, as a rule scarcely visible, was beaded with a dew of emotion. Hélène wiped her temples with the end of her striped scarf. A passionate desire to be sincere, and the odour of an irritated blonde, emanated from her, although she kept silent with all her might. She implored me to understand, not to force her to speak; but I suddenly stopped troubling about her, in so far as she was Hélène Clément. I put her into her niche in the universe, among the spectacles of other days of which I had been the anonymous spectator or the proud begetter. That decent silly creature will never know that I held her worthy to rank in my memory with my tears for my adolescent joys: the shock of my first sight of a dawn of dark fire on an iron-blue peak covered with violet snow; the flower-like unfolding of the crinkled hand of a new-born babe; the echo of a single long note taking wing from the throat of a bird, low at first, then so high that I confused it, at the moment when it broke off, with the gliding of a shooting star; and those flames, my very dear, those dishevelled peonies of flame that the fire shook over your garden. You sat down happily, spoon in hand, *"since it was nothing but straw".*

After that it's a relief to get back to Hélène, I must say. She was stammering, hampered by her uneasy love and her respectful suspicion. "So there you are!" I nearly said to her. A jilted girl doesn't have such an easy time of it. She talked of how ashamed she was, of how it was her duty to go "somewhere else", she blamed herself for having come to see me to-day and promised "never to come again, since . . ." She circled miserably round a conclusion hedged about by four or five terrible, barbed, impregnable words, "since you are the . . . the friend of Vial". For she wouldn't have dared say "the mistress".

She was soon far past that moment which had illumined the whole of her, and I watched my memories diminish, grow dim and darken.

"If you would at least say a word to me, Madame, only one word, even if it were only to throw me out. I have nothing against *you,* Madame, I swear it. . . ."

"But neither have I got anything against you, Hélène."

And then came the tears. Oh, these great galumphing girls, who don't hesitate to racket round on their own, drive their own cars, smoke coarse tobacco and abuse their father and mother!

"Come now, Hélène, come!"

As I write this, I once again experience a great feeling of repulsion for what took place this morning—it has not yet struck midnight. Only now do I dare to name the cause of my embarrassment, of my blushing and my clumsiness in articulating a few simple words: it is called timidity. When one leaves love and the practice of love behind, does that mean that one finds timidity again? Was it then so difficult to say what I finally did say to that weeping girl, begging for charity: "No, no, my child, you're imagining something extremely stupid. Nobody here is taking anything at all from anyone. I forgive you very willingly and if I can help you . . ."

This was more than the poor girl was asking for. She said "Thank you, thank you," and stammeringly extolled my "goodness" and wetted my hands with her kisses.

"Don't say '*vous*' to me, Madame, don't say '*vous*'. . . ." When I opened the door for her the setting sun enveloped the whole of her as she stood on my doorstep, with her crumpled white frock and her swollen eyes, laughing a little, moist, re-powdered, somehow touching. But I was suffering from my wretched timidity, face to face with that young Hélène in disarray. Disarray is not timidity. It is rather a kind of carelessness, a relish in letting oneself go.

My day has not been a pleasant one. I still have days and days before me, I suppose; but I no longer like spoiling them. Untimely timidity, slightly withered and bitter like anything which has been kept too long, equivocal and useless. It neither becomes me nor helps me.

A faint puff of sirocco wafts silently from one end of the bedroom to the other, ventilating the room no more than would a captive owl. When I have finished with these pages—the colour of daylight in the dark—I shall go and sleep on the raffia mattress out of doors. The whole sky wheels above the heads of those who sleep in the open, and if I wake once or twice before broad day, the course of the great stars, that I find no longer in the same place, makes me slightly giddy. Sometimes the end of the night is so cold that at three in the morning the dew traces a path of tears along the leaves, and the long hairs of my Angora blanket turn silver as a meadow. Ti-mi-di-ty, I have experienced timidity. Yet all I need have done was to speak of love and clear myself of suspicion. The thing is that fear of ridicule—even my own fear—restricts one. Can you imagine me proclaiming, with the blush of innocence on my forehead, that Vial . . .

Now I come to think of it, what about him in all this? The heroine is laying claim to all the limelight in this little story. She charges into the foreground, planting there her unambiguous colours and her unassailable respectability that is in such poor taste. And what of the man? He lies low and remains silent. What a relief!

The man in question did not remain silent for long. I was astonished to find how quickly Hélène's thoughts, travelling subtly along three hundred metres of coast and following the curves of the shore like a thirsty bird, had broken into Vial's house and his peace of mind. I didn't fail to notice that this morning, instead of opening the gate and coming out surrounded by the welcoming dogs, Vial leant against the gate and called from a distance:

"It's the pair of us, Luc-Albert Moreau and me."

And with his arm he pointed out—strangely clad in black with hands crossed, eyes as moist as those of a doe and a look as patient and gentle as a country saint —Luc-Albert Moreau.

"D'you need references, then?" I called to Vial. "Come in, the pair of you!"

But Luc-Albert wanted to be off at once because he was going to meet some new canvases and his wife, the one bringing the others.

"You'll excuse me . . . not a canvas left in the house
. . . not a canvas left in the town. Acres and acres of
ruined canvases, all daubed by the Americans and the
Czechs. I paint on the bottoms of cardboard hat-boxes.
They say it's the station's fault. Oh, that station! You
know what that station's like. . . ."

As he spoke he seemed, with his hand curved like a
shell, to be absolving and blessing all that his word
condemned.

Under the ten o'clock sun the day was still young,
thanks to a brisk breeze coming in from the bay. A
gaiety in the light, the rustling of the mulberry trees,
the cool underside of the very great heat recalled the
month of June. The rejuvenated animals roamed about
as in spring, a great nocturnal hand seemed to have
wiped away two months from the earth. Deluded and
cheered by this I finished without effort the mulching
of the tangerine trees. In the circular trench two metres
in diameter dug round their trunks I heaped seaweed
freed from salt, then I covered it over with soil that I
stamped down with my two feet as if I were treading
grapes, and the spring wind dried my sweat as I went
along.

To lift and penetrate and tear apart the soil is a
labour—a pleasure—always accompanied by an exaltation that no unprofitable exercise can ever provide.
The sight of upturned soil makes every living creature
avid and watchful. The finches followed me, pouncing
on the worms with a cry; the cats sniffed the traces of
moisture darkening the crumbling clods; my bitch, intoxicated, was tunnelling a burrow for herself with all
four paws. Where you open up the earth, even for a
mere cabbage-patch, you always feel like the first man,
the master, the husband with no rivals. The earth you
open up has no longer any past—only a future. With
my back burnt, my nose gleaming and my heart pounding with a hollow sound like a footstep behind a wall,
I was so absorbed that for a moment I forgot Vial.

Gardening rivets eyes and mind on the earth, and when a shrubby tree has been helped, nourished, supported and cosily settled in its mulch covered with fresh earth, its expression, its happy look fill me with love.

"All the same, Vial, if it were really spring, how much more fragrant the earth would smell!"

"If it were really spring . . ." repeated Vial. "But in that case we should be far from here, and shouldn't be enjoying the fragrance of this earth."

"Just wait, Vial, soon I shall be coming here in the spring, and in the autumn, and also in those months that serve to fill in the gaps between two seasons—February, say, or else the second fortnight of November. The second fortnight of November, when the vines are bare. This tiny little tangerine tree, like a ball, don't you think it has a certain style already? Round as an apple! I shall try and keep it that shape. In ten years . . ."

Some invisible, unspeakable thing must be waiting for me at the end of that time, since I faltered over the ten years and could not go on.

"In ten years?" echoed Vial.

I raised my head to answer and thought that this well-built young man, fitting so neatly inside his beautiful brown skin, made, in spite of his white garment, rather a dark patch against the pink wall, the hollyhocks, the geraniums and dahlias of my enclosure.

"In ten years, Vial, one will pick beautiful tangerines from this little tree."

"You will pick them," said Vial.

"I or someone else, that doesn't matter."

"It does," said Vial.

He looked down his rather big nose and let me lift the full watering-can without helping me.

"Don't tire yourself, Vial!"

"Sorry. . . ."

He stretched out a bronze arm and a hand whose fingers were browned by the sun. There was an appre-

ciable contrast between the strength of the arm, and
the hand with its long fingers, and I shrugged my shoulders, disdaining the help of that hand.

"Pooh!"

"Yes, I know!"

Vial knows how to supply the missing words in a
sentence and interpret an exclamation in the right way.

"I didn't . . . *think* that to hurt your feelings. When
a man's hand is slender it's rather beautiful."

"It's rather beautiful, but you don't like it."

"Not for a labourer, naturally. Oh, I feel so con-
gested I shall burst, quick, a bathe! The skin on my
back's splitting, the upper part of my arms is peeling
and as for my nose . . . Think of it, since half-past
seven this morning! I look frightful, don't I?"

Vial looked at my face and hands; the sun made
him blink as he turned his upper lip back over his
teeth. His grimace changed into a woebegone little
tremor and he answered "Yes."

It was, I admit, the one answer I wasn't expecting.
And Vial's tone of voice made it impossible for me to
make a joke of it. All the same I wanted to laugh as I
wiped my neck and forehead. "Well, my boy, you don't
exactly beat about the bush, do you?"

And I managed an awkward little feminine laugh, in
order to insist "So you find me frightful and you tell
me so?"

Vial was still staring at me, still with an expression
of intolerant suffering, and he made me wait for his
reply.

"Yes. For the past three hours you've been sticking
at this idiotic—or, if you prefer, useless—work, just
as you do every day. For three hours you've been roast-
ing in the sun, your hands are like the hands of a day-
labourer, that old overall has lost its colour and you
haven't condescended to powder your nose since this
morning. Why, why do you do it? Yes, I know you
enjoy it, that you're using up a kind of pugnacious

fury. But there are other pleasures of the same kind
—oh, I don't know, picking flowers, walking along the
shore, putting on your big white hat and knotting a
blue scarf round your neck. You have such beautiful
eyes, when you want to. And what about giving a little
thought to us who love you and who are worth just as
much as those insignificant little trees, it seems to
me . . ."

He felt his audacity petering out, and merely added,
"It's true, all that!" out of pure sulkiness, shifting the
soil with the tip of his foot.

The sun streamed down on his bronzed, well-shaven
cheek. On such a face youth ought never to be dazzling.
His chestnut-coloured eyes have depth and a flattering
fringe of dark lashes. His mouth has the advantage of
strong teeth and a groove dividing the upper lip. Vial
will enjoy a decent old age, a time of maturity when
people will say of him, looking at his long nose with
its little hump, his firm chin and prominent eyebrows:
"What a good-looking young man he must have been!"
He will answer with a sigh: "Ah, if you'd known me at
thirty! Without immodesty, I . . ." And it will not be
true.

That was what I was thinking of as I wiped the nape
of my neck and tidied my hair, in the presence of a
man who had just addressed to me, for the first time
since we had known each other, words full of hidden
meaning. Yes indeed! What do people suppose we are
thinking when we look at men—and women—we older
women confined in a precarious, solitary sort of secu-
rity, face to face with the youth of other people? It is
true that we are pitiless in our judgments; and as far as
I am concerned, if I aspire to detachment, I start
from a solid basis. I say, "You're no longer any use to
me," before I get as far as saying "So I'd like to be
useful to you myself in some way." Am I going to
devote myself to someone again? Yes, if I can't avoid
it. To a man or to a woman, and as little as possible.

But I still feel myself too fragile for a perfect, harmonious solitude, which reverberates with every shock but keeps its shape, its open calyx turned towards the living world.

All the same I was thinking of Vial as I looked at Vial and rubbed the light, sandy, salty soil off my legs. There was no need to reply at once, and perhaps I enjoyed prolonging the silence wherein I moved at my ease, *"since it was nothing but straw . . .",* and since my timidity, yesterday's ti-mi-di-ty, had vanished. O Man, friend or foe, façade that faithfully reflects and sends back to us everything that we throw at you, born interlocutor! I stepped confidently over my latest seed-bed.

"Come on then, Vial, my boy. We'll go and bathe and afterwards I've something to say to you. If you'd like to lunch with me, there are stuffed sardines."

It happened that the bathe, disturbed by the fear of sharks, brought us neither silence nor intimacy. This is the month when they stray into the bays, and up the mouths of rivers; the other day my neighbour ran his boat aground against the flank of a shark; his boat lacked draught and he found himself in a ticklish situation. The tourists of the neighbourhood, and my summer companions, about ten in number, were revelling in the contrast between the fresh weather and the warm bathe. As for the shark, we're prudent enough to fear this annual menace. When we dive, we keep our eyes open in the jellyfish-coloured, clouded crystal water, and the least, unexpected, shadow of a cloud, sailing along the sea-bed of white sand, sends us quickly back to the surface, out of breath and none too proud of ourselves. Naked, wet, and defenceless, this morning we felt as united as a group shipwrecked in the Antipodes, and some mothers were calling back their paddling children as though to shelter them from a flight of assegais and the tentacles of an octopus.

"They say," said Géraldy, half his body out of the water like a mermaid, "that *bambinos* in the Pacific play with the sharks, swimming under water and kicking them on the nose. Like this . . ."

"No!" shouted Vial. "They've misled you! There aren't any *bambinos* in the Pacific! We forbid you any demonstration! Come back on shore this minute!"

And we laughed, because it is good to laugh, and because one laughs easily in a climate where there is a real long, hot summer with soft breezes, and leisure to state with confidence: "To-morrow, and the next day too, we'll have days no different from this when the blue and golden moments glide by, days when 'suspended time stands still', merciful days where shadows come from a drawn curtain, a closed door, or leafy trees, and not from an overcast sky."

I took special notice to-day of the way in which my friends and neighbours of the bay leave me after the eleven o'clock bathe, which ends towards half-past twelve. None of the men present asked Vial, "Are you coming?" None of them suggested to him, "I'll drop you at your door, it's on my way." They knew that Vial would be lunching with me. On the days when I don't know whether Vial is lunching with me or not, they know all the same. None of them, when they went off in one direction or another towards the horns of the crescent-shaped beach, thought of stopping and looking back to see whether Vial were coming. But none of them wanted to cause me pain or irritation by saying to Vial, "Oh yes, of course, you're staying here."

Gloomily, Vial watched them depart. On other days it was only their presence that made him gloomy. A secret, well guarded by its custodians, hermetically sealed, will keep without harm, and without result. But Hélène Clément had spoken and the honourable peace was at an end. The violated secret scattered its seeds, the seeds of a secret divulged. Vial now acted like a man who has been wakened in the middle of the night, robbed of his clothes and pushed out of his own house. And I feel neither refreshed nor irritated, but a little disillusioned by my solitude. Twenty-four hours, a few words: only twenty-four more hours are needed, and a few other words, and time will resume its limpid course. There are some fortunate rivers whose silent flow is troubled only by one gurgle, a sob in the water marking the place where a submerged stone lies.

"As soon as we've had coffee, Vial, there's something I want to say to you."

For the meal itself is given over to the filtered sunlight, to the relaxation that comes from the cool bathe and lingers after it, and to the begging animals. The spots of sunlight shift slightly over the cloth; the youngest she-cat, on hind-legs against an earthenware jar, explored with her paw its garlanded paunch of pink clay.

But no sooner had coffee been served, than it so happened that the nursery-gardener appeared and had it with us.

Afterwards I steered him through the vines to where the clipped hedging of impoverished shrubs requires reinforcing with new plants if it is to provide a protective windbreak for my vines and young peach trees against the mistral. Then my afternoon nap, too long postponed, began to reassert its rights. Let anyone who has not experienced a longing for sleep on a glorious hot day in Provence, cast the first stone! It penetrates through one's forehead, drains the colour from one's eyes, and the whole body obeys it with the involuntarily tremors of a dreaming animal. And what had become of Vial! Gone, dissolved in the flamboyant torpor, drawn into the shadow of a pine or an espalier as he passed.

It was half-past three. In this climate, what care or duty can stand out against the need to sleep, to enter a cool abyss in the burning centre of the day?

Vial returned, like an overdue bill. He came back without returning, for he had done no more than drop my neighbours opposite at their house, my peaceful neighbours, who live remote among their beautifully set-out vines that keep the building speculators at a respectful distance. He returned, dressed in white, as evening fell, and as he was pretending to turn his five-horse-power car round and be off again, I called out sternly: "Well, Vial? A glass of home-made liqueur?"

He came up the path without saying a word, and as he made his way through the blue evening air, it seemed to me that this man with his head bent, the sudden chill in the air, the ordinary little house where a woman, her face difficult to make out, waited on the threshold, and the red lamp set on the balustrade, were horribly sad. Horribly, horribly sad. Let me set down these words and repeat them; let the gilded night receive them.

Horrible sad, abandoned, still warm but scarcely alive, silent because of I know not what shame. The gilded night is about to end. Between the serried stars glides a pallor that is already no longer the perfect blue of August midnights. But all is still velvet, nocturnal warmth, and the rediscovered pleasure of being awake in the midst of sleep. It is the deepest hour of the night, and not far from me my familiar creatures seem lifeless save for the rise and fall of their flanks.

Horribly sad, unbearably sad, sad enough to contract one's throat and dry up one's saliva, to inspire the lowest instincts of terror and self-protection—for was there not a single, imponderable instant, when I would have stoned the man who was coming towards me, when I would have pushed my empty wheelbarrow and thrown the rake and spade in his path? The bitch, who never growls, growled out of subtle contagion, and Vial called to her "But it's Vial!" as he would have called "Friend!" in a moment of danger.

When we entered the low, pink and blue living-room, everything came right again. I can never keep up the dramatic spell of fear, the sentimental illusion of it, for more than a moment. Vial smiled, his lip curled against his teeth, dazzled by the two lit lamps, for the days are getting shorter and the window held now only an aquarium of green sky, pierced by two or three stars throbbing irregularly.

"Oh, how comforting those lamps are," sighed Vial.

He stretched out his hands to them as though to a fire in the hearth.

"The cigarettes are in the blue pot. You've had to-day's newspapers?"

"Yes, do you want them?"

"Oh, I, you know, newspapers. . . . It was only to have news about the forest fires."

"Have there been some forest fires?"

"There always are in August."

He sat down like a visitor, lit a cigarette as if he were on the stage, while I reached under the table for the flat brick on which, with the help of a little lead hammer—a souvenir from the press of *Le Matin*,—I crack open kernels of the umbrella pine.

The jobs I don't like are those that need patience. It takes patience to write a book, and also to win over a man when he's feeling savage, to mend worn linen too and to sort the raisins for a plum cake. I would never have made either a good cook or a good wife, and I nearly always cut string instead of untying knots.

Vial, sitting sideways, looked as though he were caught in a trap, and I began patiently to untie the knots in the string.

"Does this noise of pine-nuts cracking irritate you? If you're thirsty, the water-cooler is outside there, and the lemons."

"I know, thank you."

He was vexed with me for being so unusually attentive. Stealthily he took note of the fact that I had put on new Catalan espadrilles, and that I was ceremonially garbed in an immaculate cotton frock, one of those red, white and yellow negresses' robes that brighten the coast and follow the law of the sun rather than that of

fashion. While I was eating my nuts I opened an il-
lustrated magazine; Vial smoked without stopping and
followed intently, through the window, the flight of bats
against the background of gradually darkening sky. A
block of sea, petrified and black under the sky, could
still be distinguished from the land. The evening hydroplane, preceded by the low-pitched F that it draws from
the wind, appeared carrying its red lantern among the
paler lights. The she-cat, outside, mewed to be let in,
rearing itself against the lowered mosquito-screen and
scratching it delicately like a harp-player. But Vial
laughed to see her and she disappeared, after fixing
him with a cold stare.

"She doesn't like me," sighed Vial. "Yet I'd stoop
to anything to win her. If she knew it, d'you think she'd
like me a little better?"

"You may be sure she does know."

This answer satisfied him for a few minutes, then he
sought a different reassurance, a different answer.

"Aren't the Luc-Albert Moreaus, or Segonzac the
Ravishing One, or at least somebody or other, supposed
to be coming to say good night to you, on their way
back from dinner at *Le Commerce* this evening? I
thought I'd understood . . . Or perhaps it was you who
were to have gone there . . . Aren't the Carcos . . . ? I
can't remember exactly . . ."

I looked at him sideways.

"The painters are usually asleep at this hour. Since
when have I received people in the evening? The Carcos
are at Toulon."

"Oh, good. . . ."

Secretly tired, he compromised by half reclining. His
cheek pressed against the cushions of the divan, he
automatically clutched the corner of one of them, his
eyes closed and his hand clenched, as though hanging on to a reef. What ought to be done with this
flotsam! What a problem! And then, there's the awk-
wardness of our respective ages, think of it, the dif-

ference between them! If that's what you're thinking,
how far removed you are from what actually happens
in such a case! We older women don't even think of it.
We certainly think of it less than does a mature man,
although it's entirely in order for him to flaunt his fond-
ness for tender young girls. If people realised how
lightheartedly we accept and forget our "duty as elders"!
We think of it just enough to arm ourselves with
coquetry, to pay attention to our health and our adorn-
ment, and to assume pleasing wiles—things incidentally
that are also demanded of young women. No, no, when
I write "what a problem!", I don't want some reader
later on to misunderstand. It would be wrong to imagine
"us older women" trembling and aghast in the light of
our short future, suppliants before the man we love
and overwhelmed by awareness of our position. We're
not nearly so aware as people think, thank God, and
much more gallant and simple. What is a difference of
fifteen years to us? It takes more than a trifle like that
to frighten us, just when we're getting to the stage of
reasoning about such matters with a wisdom—or a folly
—worthy of the other sex. I couldn't have chosen a
better moment for affirming this than now, when here I
am as sensible as can be, more or less a widow, tender
to my memories and determined to remain so.

When I write "we women", I don't include her who
gave me the gift of carrying the years as lightly as an
apple tree does its flowers. Listen to her telling me of a
wedding dinner.

*"In the evening, a big dinner for eighty-six people,
that's enough to show it was appalling, isn't it? If I'd
died that day it would have been from those four and a
half hours of wretched food, which I hardly touched. I
was paid a lot of compliments there. On my get-up?
Certainly not, on my youthfulness. Seventy-five . . . it's
not true, is it? Must one really soon give up being
young?"* No, no, of course not, don't give it up yet—
I've never known you anything but young, your death

saves you from growing old and even from dying, you
who are always with me. The last period of your youth,
that of your seventy-fifth year, continues still. You are
wearing a big straw hat that lived out of doors all the
year round; beneath that cloche of finely plaited straw
twinkle your roving, changeable, insatiable grey eyes,
that take on a curious lozenge shape when you are uneasy or on the alert. No more eyebrows than the Mona
Lisa, and a nose, my goodness, a nose. . . . "We have
an ugly nose" you used to say, looking at me, in more
or less the same tone of voice as: "We have a ravishing
garden." And a voice, a walk. . . . When people who
didn't know you heard your little, young-girl's step on
the stairs and your crazy way of opening a door, they
would turn round and remain speechless at seeing you
disguised as a little old lady. *Must one really give up
being young?* I don't see that that would serve any
purpose, or even be seemly. Look, my dear, at this
helpless youth, circling round a still-born hope that he
can't leave alone, and see how traditional and hard to
move he seems to us! What would you have done with
him, what ought I to do with him?

Yes, what a problem! That body hanging on to a
corner of a cushion, his modest bearing in his sad state,
his careful dissembling of it—all that lying on my
divan, what a problem! Yet another vampire, without
a doubt. That is my name for those who lay claim to
my pity. They ask nothing. "Only leave me there, in
the dark!"

Time hung heavy as it ticked by in silence. I read,
then stopped reading. On any other day I might have
supposed that Vial was asleep, for sometimes my
friends do fall asleep on my divan, after a long day's
fishing or driving or bathing, or even work, a day that
renders them speechless and charms them to sleep on
the spot. This one wasn't asleep. He was unhappy. Suffering is the first disguise, the first offensive, of the
vampire. Vial, far from happy, was pretending to rest,

and I felt stirring at the root of my being the one who
now inhabits me, lighter on my heart than I was once
in her womb. I know very well they are hers, these
stirrings of pity I don't care for. But she didn't like
them either: *"Old Champion's niece is better. It will be
a stiff job for your brother to pull her through and, as
I couldn't do anything more for the moment, I've been
begging on her behalf once again. But I haven't got the
art of doing that gracefully, because the minute I come
across people who won't give anything and only want
to feather their own nests, I get red in the face and am
more likely to slang them than flatter them.*

*"As for your cat, I go every afternoon to the Little
House to give her some warm milk and make a blaze
of shavings for her. When I haven't got anything I cook
her an egg. I don't do it because it amuses me, heavens
above, but I can never rest if I think a child or an animal is hungry. So I do what will set my mind at rest:
you know my egotism."*

That's the word! Was there ever anyone cleverer at
choosing her words? Egotism. That egotism led her
from door to door, calling out that she couldn't bear
the winter cold that was freezing some poor children in
a room with no fire. She couldn't bear it when a dog
that had been scalded by his master, the pork butcher,
could find no other remedy than to howl and writhe
outside a closed and indifferent door.

My very dear, can you see, from the summit of this
night designed for a vigil, warmer and more enriched
with gold than a velvet tent, can you see my trouble?
What would you have done in my place? You know
where those attacks of an egotism that I inherited from
you have already led me? They led you to that material
ruin in which you foundered, having given everything
away. But to have no money any longer is only one
step on the way to destitution. Undefeated by your
final poverty, you became more clear and shining the
more it ate into you. But it's by no means certain that,

at the sight of that half-reclining body, you wouldn't
have made a little detour, lifting the edge of your skirt
as you used when you passed a puddle. In your honour
I at last decided to show my strength to the young man
who was shamming sleep because he was stiff with ap-
prehension.

"Are you asleep, Vial?"

He was awake, so he didn't start.

"A bit dazed," he said, sitting up.

He smoothed his hair back, straightened his open
shirt and flannel jacket and retied his *espadrilles*. I
thought how long his nose was, and that he had that
pinched look of being caught between two swing doors
that you see on people who think they are hiding their
vexations. I didn't hurry him, well knowing that when
a man isn't sure of his shirt buttons or his shoelaces,
it's not the moment to drag him into psychology.

"Vial, I told you this morning that I had something
to say to you."

He bent his head with an oriental majesty.

"Very well, then. Vial, my dear, what wonderful
weather! Listen to the hydroplane with its F note, the
gentle wind high up between the east and the north,
breathe in the pine and mint from the little salt marsh;
its fragrance is scratching at the gate like a cat!"

Vial raised his eyelids, which he had kept lowered,
his whole face opened with surprise, revealing all his
masculine good faith, and I felt myself strong in the
presence of this creature full of innocence, unversed in
the artifice of speech.

"Have you seen the grapes on the vines, Vial? Have
you noticed that the clusters are already huge and
turning blue, so close-set that a wasp couldn't squeeze
between them? D'you realise that we shall have to
gather them before the fifteenth of September? What
d'you bet that the season'll run its course before the
storms get past *Les Maures,* where the mountain is
gathering them together like balloons at the end of a

string? It's raining in Paris, Vial. It's raining at Biarritz and Deauville too. Everything is mildewy in Brittany, and the Dauphiné is covered with mushrooms. Only Provence . . ."

While I was speaking he narrowed his eyes and his whole face hardened. A living being is an endless occupation. All that this one now surrendered to me was a wary glimpse of himself. Being a man, he fears irony. Despising melancholy, he was now merely perplexed, and stiff.

"D'you understand me, Vial? It's a very lovely time of the year that I'm spending here. It's also, I assure you, a very lovely time of my life. D'you like these months that you're spending here?"

By imperceptible movements Vial's features again became the face of a brave man to whom the power to use his courage has been restored.

"No," he answered, "I don't like them. I wouldn't exchange them for anything in the world, but I don't like them. Not only have I hardly done a stroke of work all this time, but worse still I'm not happy."

"I thought you were designing an *'ensemble'* for . . ."

"For the *Quatre Quartiers*. Yes I am. My models are ready. It's a big job. Living-rooms, bedrooms, dining-room, the whole house. I'm using every penny I've got, and even a bit more, to make my models in wood and metal. But if I succeed, it means I shall be the director of the modern furniture workshops at the *Quatre Quartiers*."

"You've never told me so much about it before."

"That's true. You're not much interested in modern furnishing."

"At least I'm interested in what concerns my friends."

Vial settled himself on the divan with the movement of a horseman getting a grip on his saddle.

"Madame, I don't for a moment flatter myself that I'm your friend. You have scores of friends like me that you greet familiarly in your cheerful holiday mood."

"You're modest."

"I'm clear-sighted. It's not very difficult."

He spoke in an even, respectful voice, with an open look on his face, while his large and certainly beautiful eyes looked frankly either into mine or at some other part of my person.

"It's true, Vial, that I'm more familiar than quick to make friends. But where friendship is concerned, is there so much hurry? We should have become friends . . . later on. I know you very little."

He made a quick gesture with his hand to efface my words.

"Oh Madame, please, please!"

"You called me Colette yesterday."

"In front of people, yes, so as to seem one of the anonymous crowd. If you paid any attention to me you'd know that I've never once called you by your name when we were alone. And we've been alone together very often, since the first of July."

"Yes, I know."

"By the tone of those three words, Madame, I see we're arriving at the matter that concerns us."

"At the matter that concerns you."

"Anything that's disagreeable to you, Madame, certainly does concern me more than anything."

At that point we stopped for a moment, for the unexpected rapidity of our replies had brought us to what sounded like a quarrel.

"Gently, Vial, gently! Now, shoulders steady, and then all of a sudden . . ."

He smiled because I did.

"Accused people sometimes decide to 'come clean' because they know they'll be condemned. And then they'll talk about their crime as easily as about their first love, or the baptism of their little sister—it doesn't matter what."

He cracked the joints of his clasped fingers between his knees and questioned me urgently.

"Madame, what do you want of me? Or rather, what don't you want? I'm certain already that you're going to ask me the thing that will be hardest for me, and that I'll do whatever you want."

How men's nobility, even when it consists of nothing but words, pulls us up short! The feminine tendency to dress a man up as a hero, when he talks of sacrificing his emotional comfort, is still very strong in me.

"Good. So there won't be any difficulty. Hélène Clément . . ."

"No, Madame, not Hélène Clément."

"What d'you mean, not Hélène Clément?"

"What I say, Madame. Not Hélène Clément. Enough of Hélène Clément. Something else."

"But do try and understand me. Listen. You don't even know . . . She came yesterday and I had no difficulty in finding out for certain . . ."

"Bravo, Madame! That does credit to your perspicacity. You found out for certain? I'm delighted. Let's speak no more of it."

A sharp little light shone in Vial's eyes, and he stared at me impertinently. When he saw that I was going to get angry, he placed his hands on mine.

"No, Madame, let's speak no more of it. You want to let me know that Hélène Clément loves me, that my indifference distresses her, that I ought to feel pity and even love for that 'beautiful healthy young girl'— Géraldy's expression—and marry her? Good. I know it. It's finished. Let's speak no more of it."

· I withdrew my hands.

"Oh, if you take it like that, Vial . . ."

"Yes, Madame, I take it like that and, what's much more, I reproach you for having dragged the name of this young girl into our conversation. You had a reason for doing so? What reason? Say it! Say it, then! You take an interest in this young girl? You know her well?

You've undertaken to be responsible for the future and even for the happiness of a frail creature who's hardly twenty-six years old? Are you so fond of her? Are you her friend? Answer, Madame, answer more quickly! Why don't you answer more quickly? Because I don't give you time? It doesn't take long, Madame, to answer 'yes' whole-heartedly to all my questions, and as a rule you're prompt. You don't like Hélène Clément and, if you'll forgive the expression, you don't care a damn about her happiness, which in any case doesn't in the least concern you. Don't get angry, it's settled, it's finished. *Ouf!* I'd be glad of a glass of lemonade and I'll prepare one for you. Don't move."

He poured out our drinks and added: "Apart from that I repeat that I'll do what you like. I'm listening."

"I'm sorry. It was you who spoke of 'coming clean'."

"It would be unpardonable of me, Madame, to prevent you from continuing your rhapsody on the beauties of summer."

Ah, if I had but felt a beating of the heart, a prophetic coldness of the hands, those preliminary symptoms of distress in every part of the body! If I know myself aright, it was then and not later that I regretted the absence between us of that supreme intruder, desire. If it had been present I should, I think, have been easily able to draw from it the meaning of our meeting that evening, the spice and the danger which it lacked. It seemed to me also too obvious that Vial wanted to stress the contrast between the young companion of yesterday, the "my little Vial" who was one of a band of summer comrades, and the completely self-contained lover.

"I've already noticed, Vial, that we don't need many words to understand each other."

It was an ambiguous compliment, and went deeper than I had meant.

"Truly?" said Vial. "Truly? You really think that? To how many men in your life have you said some-

thing like that? Perhaps you've only said it to me? I
must say I haven't noticed a sign of it in any of your
books . . . no, not in any. What you've just said is
quite unlike that contempt for love that in reading you
one is always slightly aware of in your love for love.
It isn't a thing that you would have said to one of the
men who . . ."

"We're not concerned with my books here, Vial."

I couldn't hide from him the jealous discourage-
ment, the unjust hostility that seizes me when I realise
that people expect to find me true to life in the pages
of my novels.

"You must allow me the right to hide myself in them,
even if it's only in the 'stolen letter' manner. Now let's
get back to what does concern us."

"Nothing concerns both of us together, Madame, and
that makes me very sad. You've taken it into your
head to plant a third person between yourself and me.
Send her away and we shall be alone."

"But it's because I promised her . . ."

Vial threw up his hands, so dark against his white
cuffs.

"So that's what it is! You promised her! Promised
what? Frankly, Madame, what are you up to in this?"

"Not so loud, Vial, Divine's sleeping in the hut in
the vineyard. The little Clément girl told me that last
year, in this very place, you exchanged words that led
her to believe . . ."

"Very likely," said Vial. "This year it's different,
that's all."

"That's not very gallant."

Vial turned towards me abruptly.

"Why isn't it? What would not be gallant would be
if, having changed my own mind, I hadn't warned her.
I've neither run away with a minor nor slept with a
decent girl. Is that all you have to reproach me with?
Was it in honour of that insipid creature that you sang
your hymn in praise of summer? Was it with an eye to

Hélène Clément's happiness that you decided—for you have decided it—to banish me? Why do you choose to send away the one who cares most for you and understands you best? Is that the promise you made to Hélène Clément? In the name of what did she get it out of you? Of the 'correct thing'? Or of the difference in our ages? She's quite capable of it!" he cried with a note of harsh gaiety in his voice.

With a nod of denial I gave him my most affectionate look. Poor Vial, what a confession! So it was he who was thinking, was he, of the difference in our ages? What a confession of torments, of silent debates!

"Must I confess it to you, Vial? I never think about differences in ages."

"Never? What, never?"

"What I mean is . . . I just don't think about it. Any more than about the opinion of imbeciles. And that isn't the promise I gave Hélène. Vial"—I laid the flat of my hand, as I often do with him, on his swelling chest—"is it true then that you've become attached to me?"

He lowered his eyelids and compressed his lips.

"You've become attached to me in spite, as you say, of the difference in our ages. If there were no other barrier between us, I assure you that wouldn't count for much in my eyes."

With his chin he made a very slight shy movement towards my hand spread on his chest, and promptly replied.

"I'm not asking you anything. I shan't even ask you what it is you call another barrier. I'm even astonished to hear you speaking so . . . so naturally of . . . of these things that concern you."

"It's very necessary to speak of them, Vial. What I made plain to Hélène Clément was only—and in any case very vaguely—that I wasn't an obstacle between you and her, and that I never should be one."

Vial's expression changed, and with the back of his arm he pushed my hand away from his chest.

"That beats all," he cried in a choking voice. "What a lack of awareness! To associate yourself . . . To put yourself on the same plane as she! To pose as a generous rival! Rival of whom? Why not of a shop-girl? It's incredible! You, Madame, you! To put yourself, to behave like an ordinary woman, you that I'd like to see, oh, I don't know . . ."

With his raised hand he assigned me a lofty niche in the air, a kind of pedestal, and I interrupted him with an irony that pained me.

"Vial, let me stay among the living for a bit longer. I'm quite comfortable here."

"Oh, Madame. . . ."

Vial gazed at me, speechless with reproach and grief. With a swift movement he leant his cheek against my bare upper arm and closed his eyes.

"Among the living?" he repeated. "Why the ashes, even the ashes of these arms would be warmer than any living flesh. They would remain an encircling necklace still."

I had no need to break the contact, for he himself broke it immediately, to make me pleased with him. I was pleased, and I nodded approvingly at him as I watched him. I saw weariness, and a blue-black film creeping over his cheeks because of the lateness of the hour. Thirty-five or six, neither ugly, nor unwholesome, nor wicked. I was being swallowed up by the airless night during the passage of those hours when all the world is asleep, and there emanated from this lightly clad and emotionally overwrought youth an odour of amorous midnight that little by little began to make me feel sad.

"What keeps you going, Vial, apart from me? You understand what I mean?"

"Very little keeps me going, Madame, very little— and you."

"That isn't much of a portion for you."

"That's for me to say."

I got angry.

"But, you obstinate brute, where do you think you're going, where were you off to without saying a word, now that you've made a habit of me?"

"As a matter of fact I haven't the slightest idea," he answered carelessly. "The truth is I've thought of it as little as possible. Sometimes in Paris, when you hadn't time to see me, I used to think . . ."

He smiled to himself, already absorbed by the longing to describe himself, to come out into the open.

"I used to think: 'So much the better, if I don't see her I'll get more quickly over the longing to see her. I've only got to be patient, and when I go back to her she'll suddenly be sixty or seventy and then life will become possible and even agreeable again.' "

"I see. And then?"

"And then? And then when I went back to see you it happened to be a day when all your demons were awake, and you'd put on powder, made up your eyes, slipped into a new frock and could talk of nothing but travels, the theatre and playing *Chéri* on tour, planting vines and peach trees and buying a little car. And I had to begin all over again. It's the same here too," he ended, more slowly.

Throughout the silence that followed, nothing from outside disturbed the immobility of all things. In the beam from the lamp the cat, lying in the hollow of the *chaise-longue* on the terrace, announced the approach of the dew by rolling herself into a ball and the creaking of the wicker resounded as though under a vault.

Vial questioned me with his eyes as if it were my turn to say something. But what could I have added to his deep, melancholy contentment? No doubt he knew I was moved. I was. I made only one sign, which he interpreted as meaning, "Go on . . ." and an almost feminine expression, full of seduction, passed over his features, as if his whole, brown, masculine face were going to break up and reveal a dazzling countenance; but it did not last. It was only the flash of a semblance of triumph, of a spark of happiness. Come now, I must act quickly and rather sternly, to undeceive this decent man. Swifter than I, he plunged in deeper.

"Madame," he went on, restraining himself from speaking with heat, "I haven't much more to say to you. I never have had much to say to you. No one is more devoid of second thoughts—I might almost add 'of desires'—than I."

"Yes, there's me."

"Forgive me, but I can't believe you. You invited me this evening . . ."

"Yesterday evening."

He passed his hand over his cheek and became embarrassed to find it stubbly.

"Oh, how late it is! You invited me yesterday evening, and yesterday morning you . . . summoned me. Was it only to talk to me about the little Clément girl? And of the fact that you felt it your duty to get rid of me?"

"Yes. . . ."

I hesitated, and he rebelled.

"What else is there, Madame? I beg you not to get it into your head that I must be managed and treated carefully. I'd rather confess to you that I'm not even unhappy. Truly not. Up to now I've felt like someone carrying on his person something very fragile. Every day I breathed again, 'Still nothing broken to-day!' There never would have been anything broken, Madame, if the rather heavy and perhaps not very well-intentioned hand of an outsider . . ."

"Oh come now, leave the child alone."

As soon as I heard my words I was ashamed of them. I still feel ashamed of them as I write them down. They were the words, and the tone of voice, of a

mawkish rival, of a perfidious stepmother. It was the
inveterate homage, the mean acquiescence which comes
out of us when man solicits it, man, that luxury, that
choice game, the most rare male. Vial imprudently
glittered with joy, like a fragment of glass in the moonlight.

"But I do leave her alone, Madame, I've never
wanted to do anything else! I'm not asking anything
of anyone, *I*'m not! I'm so nice, so easy. . . . Listen,
Madame, if you were to suggest to me, you yourself,
that I should change, that . . . that I should improve
my lot, I should be capable of crying 'Rubbish!' and
even *'Vade retro!'* "

And he burst out laughing—all by himself. He had
overshot his capacity. A grown man can hardly ever
play the urchin with impunity. Besides, in order to be
attractive when he acts caddishly, he must have a
deeply engrained evil streak, the gift of improvisation,
or at least the light touch that some mediocre Satans
achieve—all virtues which extreme youth has no difficulty in making up for.

Was the honest Vial, by making himself cheap like
a little middle-class girl going on the streets out of
despair, perhaps trying, in order to please me, to con-
form to a type of man he had discovered in three
hundred pages of mine, in which I celebrate slightly dis-
honourable masculine immunities? If so, it might have
made me smile. But like the night, I was beginning to
throw off languor and would soon emerge from the
shadows. Through the door came a coldness bred of
the clash between a young breeze and yesterday's air,
heated by our two bodies. The flagstone of the threshold gleamed as though under rain, and the ragged ghost
of the big eucalyptus gradually loomed up against the
sky again.

Vial was mistakenly hoping that his passivity would
win the day. That's not an uncommon tactic with
men—rather the reverse. Vial belongs to a category of

lovers that, in the course of my amorous life, I have merely glimpsed from a distance of my own choosing. He must be a bit dull all day long, but when dusk falls he shines and becomes apt for love, pleasing during love-making as young peasants are, and workmen in the flower of their youth. I could see him, I could indeed, as if I were there.

Vial swiftly put a woollen scarf round my shoulders, though I had not shivered.

"Is that all right? You'll be warm enough? The day will soon be here, Madame. It can be my witness that I never hoped to see it dawn alone with you in your house. Let me at least be proud of that, if not happy. I often sin through pride, as happens with people of lowly origin who are disgusted with the milieu to which they were born. Disgusted . . . that's it, I was born disgusted. My war-time comrades joked about my disgust for ordinary women and commonplace adventures. A prince couldn't be more disgusted than I. It's comic, isn't it?"

"No," I said absently.

"If you knew," he went on in a lower tone, "it's only here that I've lived through such long days. Of all the things in you that have helped me, none is so precious as that colour that your even temper gives to the days, the savour they acquire by gliding over you. In spite of a kind of mannishness, a hail-fellow-well-met manner which you only put on. . . ."

I did not interrupt him. A dull blue light lay on his forehead and the hollows of his cheeks, the orange-coloured lamps grew red under the insinuating progress of the blue. In the enclosed garden a bird freed itself from the night with a cry so long, so divorced from melody, that it gave me the illusion of tearing myself from sleep. Dark in his white garments, curled up in the hollow of the divan, Vial still belonged lazily to the night, and in order to see him better I made use of a former self of mine who awoke in me with the day, a self that enjoyed physical exchanges and was expert at discerning promise in the shape of a body. The nakedness of the daily bathe had made the contours of this particular body familiar to me: the Egyptian shoulders, the strong cylindrical neck, and above all the lustre, the rare and mysterious signs that confer on certain men a grade in the voluptuous hierarchy, in the animal aristocracy. So—feeling I hadn't much time— I hastened to breathe in through all my pores the warmth that came to me from a forbidden spectacle *"since it was nothing but straw . . ."*

"When one is fortunate enough to return from the war in such a commonplace way, with two scars on the arm, all one asks for afterwards is to live fully and work hard. But my father . . ."

What is it that he lacks, then? What disturbance, what drama of gestation, of growth? He has nothing in common with the people I've known, whose stammerings have communicated themselves to me when I've held them in my arms and looked down at them.

"To want everything, to be aware of everything, at the bottom of one's heart to lay claim to everything, is a great misfortune for a young man who is obliged to live in a mediocre way, and who didn't know that one day he would have the luck to be listened to by you."

Yes. But there is no chance that his appearance, his effort to join me, even his suffering could convey to me the torture of the seed beneath the soil, the torment of the plant in such a hurry to flower, since that is its duty, that it lacerates itself in the process. I've known, then lost, beings who swore—it was their way of testifying to my power—that they would perish if I did not release them from themselves, that they would never blossom if I refused them their only climate: my presence. But this one had already flowered, and lost his flowers, more than once.

". . . and I'm not ashamed to let you see that I'm

more astonished and poorer in memories than if life had just begun for me. . . ."

Yes. But it hasn't just begun for you. That's only a manner of speaking. You can't deceive me about that, even by playing on your innocence. We older women, when our last, valiant combats are over, are generally concerned only with the worst or the best; there's no great merit in discerning that you are neither the one nor the other. I'm thinking of my future, whose hours may be counted. If I were to enter the lists again, that future would be entirely given over to burning truths, to bitternesses more cruel than all—or else to duels where each side wants to outstrip the other in pride. You are marked out for an easier destiny, Vial, than trying to outstrip me in pride.

"Dear Valère Vial!"

I hoped that this cry would release me from that privileged place where it was for me to choose whether to wound or to help.

"I'm here, Madame, I'm here! In fact that is my greatest crime."

Stiff from his long watch, he got up and stretched, obliterating all his angles. His beautiful summer livery, polished and brown, looked soiled on the cheeks by the stiff stubble that pierced the skin. The brilliant white of his eyes was less clear than yesterday. Without a night's sleep, or any attention, what was my face looking like? I think of it to-day, I didn't think of it yesterday. All I thought of was to seal, with a wound or an embrace, the night that was over at last. A couple absorbed in each other doesn't know what a brief conversation is. How endless are those discussions in which those who are not true lovers flounder!

The sour scent of some peaches, forgotten in a bowl, reminded me of their existence. I bit into one and suddenly I was hungry and thirsty again for the round material world, crammed with savours: in a few moments boiling milk, black coffee, and the butter lying at the bottom of the well would fulfil their healing office.

"Dear Valère Vial, you diverted me from what I had begun to say to you a moment . . ."—I playfully pointed out to him one of the last stars, pale yellow, which had stopped its scintillating dance—"a moment ago."

"You have only to go on, Madame. Or to begin again, I'm still here."

Was this sincere friendship, or a pretence of friendship? From the pleasure that I derived from his friendly voice, I realised that this sleepless night had told on my strength.

"Vial, I wanted to talk to you as to an affectionate human being—if there are human beings that are affectionate."

My reservation came at the right moment: Vial jibbed at the word spurned by all lovers, and his look took back the trust he had reposed in me.

"I told you that I was spending here a beautiful time of the year, but above all a beautiful time of my life. This is a fairly recent state of affairs, as my friends know."

He remained silent, as if dried-up.

"So that I don't always feel very sure of myself in this new state. Sometimes I am forced to ask myself—when all of a sudden I go in for great activity, such as spring-cleaning, insensate gardening, or a move—if it's because of this new lightness or the remains of old fever. D'you understand?"

He nodded "yes", but showed me the face of a stranger, and it didn't occur to me then that he might be suffering.

"To make a clean sweep, to build up once more, to be born again has never been too much for me. But to-day it's no longer a question of making a clean sweep, it's a question of beginning something I have never done. So understand, Vial, that this is the first

time since I was sixteen that I'm going to have to live—
or even die—without my life or death depending on
love. It's so extraordinary. You can't know. You have
time."

Vial, unconcern stamped all over him, stubborn from
head to foot, silently refused to understand or help me
out. I felt very tired, ready to recoil before the crimson
invasion that was rising from the sea, but I also wanted
to end this night honourably—the word suggested itself
to me and I couldn't get rid of it.

"You see, in future my sadness, if I'm sad, and my
gaiety, if I'm gay, must exist without the motive which
has been all they needed for thirty years: love. I've
nearly got there. It's prodigious. It's so prodigious.
When a woman has just given birth to a child, a reflex
action sometimes makes her cry out again on waking
from her first sleep after deliverance. And I, you see,
still have the reflex of love, I forget that I have put
aside the fruit I once produced. I don't struggle against
it, Vial. Sometimes I cry inside myself: 'Oh dear, provided He's still there!' and sometimes: 'Oh dear, provided He's no longer there!' "

"Who?" asked Vial, naïvely.

I began to laugh, and patted the beautiful chest that
his open shirt exposed to the morning wind and to my
hand—my hand that is older than I, though at that
hour I must certainly have looked my age.

"No one, Vial, no one. No one any longer. But I am
not dead, far from it, nor insensible. I can be hurt. You
could hurt me. You're not the kind of man to be satisfied with that?"

A long hand with thin fingers, swift as a paw, seized
mine.

"I could still make do with that," he muttered.

It was only a passing threat. I was grateful to Vial
for such an avowal, I relished the slightly outrageous
form, the direct and obvious source of it. I withdrew
my hand gently, shrugged my shoulders and tried to
make him ashamed, as I would a child.

"Oh, Vial! What end do you think would await us if I listened to you?"

"What end?" he repeated. "Oh, of course. Why, your end—or mine. I admit," he added complacently, "yes, I admit there were times when I shouldn't have minded if you'd died."

I found no answer to so time-honoured a wish. A slight quiver of his eyeballs, a vague laugh showed me that Vial might still be thinking of acting the desperate lover and I began to be pettily afraid lest anyone should discover this dishevelled boy on my doorstep. There was no time to be lost, the day was upon us, the first whirring swallows were encircling the roof. Only a long Chinese junk of clouds, thick red-violet in colour and anchored flush with the horizon, delayed the first fire of dawn. With a great roll of hollow, singing thunder, a wagon on the coast road proclaimed that it was transporting empty barrels. Vial turned up the collar of his white jacket round his yesterday's beard and the brown face that sleeplessness and starvation were turning green. He shifted his weight from one foot to the other, as though he were trampling snow, and he gazed for a long time at the sea, my house and two empty seats on the terrace.

"Well then . . . *au revoir,* Madame."

"*Au revoir,* dear Vial. You . . . I shan't see you at lunch-time?"

He took this for an excess of hostile precaution, and was hurt.

"No. Nor to-morrow. I must go to Moustier-Sainte-Marie, and from there to some little places strung along about two hundred kilometres of the coast. To buy some Provençal counterpanes for my shop in Paris, and some Varages plates that I've been told about."

"Yes. But this isn't an 'eternal farewell'! We'll see each other again, Vial?"

"As soon as I can, Madame."

He seemed pleased to have answered so well in so few words, and I let him go. His little car started up discreetly in the deep white dust of the dry road. Then the cat appeared, like a fairy, and I went into the kitchen to light the fire without waiting for Divine, for I was trembling with cold and all I felt was an urgent need to soak myself in a very hot, vinegary, aromatic bath, a bath like those in which one takes refuge in Paris, on black winter mornings.

WE SETTLERS, SCATTERED ALONG THE COAST, ENJOY
impromptu dinners because they bring us together for
an hour or two but do not violate the peace of our
dwellings, the privacy of our summer life, which does
not include afternoon reunions or five o'clock teas. The
protocol of the season demands that a sudden unani-
mous whim, rather than friendly planning, should regu-
late our relations. If we get an invitation for a week
ahead we are hesitant and evasive: "Oh, I don't know
if I'm free. It just happens that the Gignoux boy has to
take us to La Seyne. . . ." Or else we're working, or
we're "just" planning a picnic in the forest, to feed off
poached game.

As a rule it happens that a single voice, we don't
know whose in advance, expresses our desire for brief
sociability. It may be that of the Great Dédé, or Dorny's
little nasal pipe, or the ravenous yawn of Daragnès
sighing: "How empty I feel . . ." And it can't happen
until half-past seven has struck on the bulbous belfry,
until the last spark of the setting sun, dancing on the
bellies of the siphons, is reflected in Segonzac's green,
sorcerer's eyes, and until a vague smell of bread comes
from the pink façades along the quay, warmer than the
cooling air. Only then does a nonchalant voice speak
up. "I wonder what there is to eat at *La Lyonnaise's?*"

No one has moved, yet the reply comes, surprisingly
precise. "Nothing. Tomatoes, and the local ham."

"We've got a big Bologna sausage and some fine gorgonzola," murmurs another sweet voice, which belongs to the violinist Morhange. "But that wouldn't be enough for everyone."

"And I suppose *my* soup of *my* onions, *gratiné,* is just so much goat dung?" cries Thérèse Dorny, or Suzanne Villebœuf.

At this point Segonzac rises to his feet, doffing his ancient felt hat: "My good sirs, my good ladies, could it be that a jaunt as far as my house would frighten you off? I'm only a simple peasant, I have what I have but, faith of a churl, I have my heart on my hand and my hand everywhere."

While the Ravishing One is still at his favourite game of imitations, silent feet, shod with *espadrilles,* have been running hither and thither until, loaded with local ham, tomatoes and peaches, cheeses, almond tarts, sausages shaped like a club, long breads that we hug as if they were stolen children, and a hot soup-tureen tied up in a napkin, we take to the rutty hill road in two or three cars. The exercise is familiar to us: twenty minutes later a table set up under a wattle roof offers us a feast, and the green moonlight of old starboard lights, hung high in the branches, streams unctuously over the convex leaves of the magnolias.

That is how we were yesterday evening, at the top of the hill. The inlet of sea, away below, kept a milky clarity that no longer came from the sky. We made out the motionless lights of the port and their trembling reflections. Above our heads, between two torches, swung a long bunch of ripening grapes, and one of us picked a green one.

"The vintage will be early, but scanty."

"My farmer says that we shall make ten hectos, all the same," states Segonzac with pride. "What about you, Colette?"

"I'm reckoning on a third of the crop, it hasn't rained enough and mine are very old vines: eighteen hundred to two thousand."

"Two thousand what?"

"Litres; but I only have half of it for myself."

"God's death, my good girl, you'll turn into a wine merchant!"

"A thousand litres!" sighed Suzanne Villebœuf, quite overcome, as if she were condemned to drink the lot.

She was wearing a frock with sprays of flowers on a black ground, peasant stuff from Italy, which she had cut in the style of old Provence, and no one could explain why she looked as though she were disguised as a gipsy.

The air smelt of eucalyptus and over-ripe peaches. Silkworm moths and the delicate butterflies of the gooseberry bushes crackled as they got burnt in the shades of the electric lights. Hélène Clément patiently rescued the least hurt on the end of a pickle-fork, and then out of pity gave them to the cat.

"Oh, a shooting star!"

"It fell on Saint-Raphael."

We had finished eating, and almost finished talking. A big jug of ordinary greenish glass, with a jutting navel, was passed lazily round the table and tilted to fill our glasses again with a good wine from Cavalaire, a young wine with an after-taste of cedar wood, whose warm vapour awakened a few wasps. Our sociability, now that it was satisfied, was on the point of giving place, according to the swing of the pendulum, to our unsociability. The painters, tired out with sun, would have given way to a childlike torpor, but their wives, who had rested after lunch in a harem-like peace, turned longing eyes towards the bay and hummed under their breath.

"After all," one of them risked, "it's only a quarter to ten."

"Waltz, pretty maidens!" sang a timid soprano, and then stopped short.

"If Carco were here . . ." said another voice.

"Carco doesn't dance. What we need is Vial."

Whereupon there fell a very short silence and Luc-

Albert Moreau, afraid I might be hurt, cried: "It's true, it's true, we need Vial! But since he isn't here, you see . . . Well, he isn't here, that's all!"

"He's preparing his white exhibition, and his sale of household articles," said Thérèse contemptuously. As she was trying to rent an "amusing" little *boutique,* she envied Vial his Parisian shop.

"He's at Vaison, behind Avignon," said Hélène Clément.

My friends looked at her sternly.

She kept her eyes down and went on feeding grilled moths to the black cat on her knee, that looked like a conger eel.

"That's enough to make it burst," Morhange pointed out to her vindictively. "Isn't it, Madame Colette?"

"Oh, no, why? They're fat, and roasted. Naturally I wouldn't grill butterflies for cats on purpose, but you can't prevent silkworm moths from flying at the electric lights."

"Nor women from going dancing," sighed a tall land-scape painter, getting up. "Come on, let's go and have a hop at Pastecchi's. But we'll go home early?"

One of the young women threw out a "Yes!" as piercing as the whinny of a mare, headlights ranged over the vines, striking here and there a vine-stock of quicksilver, a dog white as salt, a livid terrified rose-bush. Seeing Luc-Albert grovelling like a suppliant before an ancient and obstinate little car, Thérèse Dorny threw at him in passing, "Won't your stove draw to-night?" and our laughter descended the hill, carried by silent cars in neutral gear.

As we drew nearer to the sea, the bay became more thickly starred. I felt the bare arm of Hélène Clément against my bare arm. Since the departure of Vial, I had only seen her on the quay, in the bookshop, at market time, at lemonade time, and never alone. In the first days of the week she had shown me an eagerness, a deference as much as to say: "Well? Well? What have you been doing? What news?" to which I had answered

nothing. She was, I thought, resigned, and was thinking—but how could I have thought so?—of other
things. Her bare arm, in the shadow, gave under mine.

"Madame Colette, you know," whispered Hélène, "I
only know it by a post-card."

"Know what, my child?"

"And it's a post-card from my mother, who's with
father at Vaison, staying with my grandmother
Clément," she went on, passing over my question. "Our
families know each other. But I thought I couldn't
say it just now . . . that it was better . . . I wasn't able
to consult you about it before dinner."

I pressed the bare arm, cool as the evening.

"It was better."

And I was astonished that she should know so well
what is better, what is less good, I admired her face
full of plans and hopes for events, arrivals, embarka-
tions.

When night has fallen, reducing the sea to its language of lapping waves, noises like sucking lips, and
obscure gnawings between the bellies of the moored
boats, the marine immensity to a little black wall, low
and vertical against the sky, the outrageous blue and
gold of the day to the lights of the jetty, trade to the
two cafés and a little night-prowling bazaar, then we
discover that our port is just a little port. As we passed
by, a foreign yacht, in a good position flush with the
quay, was shamelessly displaying its brasses, its electric-
ity, its bridge of West Indian wood, its dining table
surrounded by men naked to the waist and women in
low frocks with great ropes of pearls, its immaculate
waiters. We stopped to contemplate the magnificent ark
that the sea had brought and that the sea would take
away, when those people had thrown overboard their
last fruit-peeling and decked the water with their floating newspapers.

"Hi, you there, chuck us some cigarettes," a down-
at-heel boy called to them.

One of the passengers on view turned round to eye the child perched on the gangway, and did not answer.

"Hi, all of you, what time do you make love? If it's late, I'm afraid I won't be able to wait till then."

He fled, rewarded by our laughter.

A hundred metres further on, in the crook of the jetty, Pastecchi has his dance-hall and bar. It's a good corner, sheltered from the wind. It's beautiful because its view embraces at the same time a section of imprisoned sea, the *tartanes* adorned with painted stripes and the flat houses on their splayed bases, of tender lilac and dove-pink.

An exhausted little man, who looks lazy but rarely rests, stands guard over the bareness of a rectangular hall, as though he had been ordered to keep any decoration away from it. There's not a festoon to be seen on the walls, nor a bunch of flowers on the corner of the counter, no fresh colour anywhere, not even a paper frill round the electric bulbs. As in a mortuary chapel for the poor, it is on the catafalque that a display of flowers and superfluity is amassed. What I call the catafalque is the ancient mechanical piano, stricken in years and black as an old tail-coat. But there isn't one of its panels that doesn't frame, in wistaria and blue ribbons, Venice, the Tyrol, a lake in moonlight, or Cadiz, painted in lifelike colours. It swallows, through a slit of a mouth edged with brass, counters worth twenty centimes, and gives them back a hundredfold in metallic polkas and *javas* made of lustreless tin, full of big gaps of consumptive-sounding silences. It is a hollow music, of such a dismal severity that we couldn't bear it without dancers. As soon as the first measures precipitate into the coffer a rhythmical shower of old coins, bits of glass and lead combs, a couple, two couples, ten couples of dancers revolve obediently, and when you don't hear hemp soles sliding, you're aware of the silky rustle of bare feet.

When I write dancers, I refer to men and not girls. At the Jetty these are a negligible minority. Pretty, bold, and with shaven necks, they learn from the tourist the chic of sunburnt legs and the incomparable scarf. But when a "foreign woman" comes to the dance in the evening in *espadrilles,* the local girls wear patent leather slippers on their bare feet.

We all crowd together on the wobbly wooden benches, round a cracked marble table. Even so some young workmen from the factory and two sailors, in order to make room for us, have to move back their tom-cat loins and their glasses of *pastis.* Hélène Clément clamped her bare shoulder, her hip and her long leg against a young sea animal, polished like precious wood, with the confidence of a girl who had never found herself in the middle of a deserted road, three steps away from a silent, motionless, unknown man with swinging arms. Some men take for impudence, in Hélène, what is only persistent purity. She got up promptly and went off to waltz in the arms of a blue sailor, who danced as the youths do here, that is to say without speaking, clasping his partner in a close and impersonal embrace and holding high his face, which revealed nothing.

Around this beautiful couple turned, under the cruel glare of the execrable lighting, a few habitués of the coast: two Swedes—husband and wife, brother and sister?—all pale red from ankles to hair, some massive Czechs, their bodies hardly hewn out of the block, two or three new-style German women, thin, half-naked, swarthy and hot on the eye—so many coloured stains against a dark background of shirtless adolescents in thin black sweaters tight round the neck, sailors blue as the night, and ruddy-bronze, thickset stevedores of *tartanes,* light on their feet, heroes of the dance. They were waltzing with each other under the impure gaze of a public come a long way to see them. Two friends, like as twins in their stature, their slender feet and the similarity of their smiles, who hadn't condescended the whole summer to invite a "bitch from Paris", came to rest near us, accepted from the great Dédé, who admired them, a bottle of fizzy drink, answered, to an indiscreet question, "We two dance together because the girls don't dance well enough", and went off to entwine their arms and mingle their knees again.

A frantic brunette with straight hair, in a yellow fichu, come just as she was, in a car, from a neighbouring shore, was rubbing stomachs with an aloof workman who, though he held her by the loins, seemed not to see her. A charmer of a dark young man, in a torn shirt of grey flannelette, who seemed riveted to another young man, delicate, empty and immaterial, the whiter because of a red silk handkerchief, tied tight high up round his neck, under the ear, threw us glances of defiance as he passed, and a hammer-shaped mulatto— huge shoulders and a waist that could have fitted into a garter—carried against his heart, feet off the ground, a child almost asleep with so much gyrating, who let his head flop and his arms hang limp.

No other noise beyond the clink of coins, crockery and dominoes, all blended together with that of the mechanical piano. One doesn't come to the Jetty to talk, nor even to get drunk. At the Jetty one dances.

The open windows let in the smell of the melon rinds floating on the water of the port; between two parts of a tango, a long sigh announced that a wave, born far out at sea, had just died within a few paces of us.

The young women with me watched the male couples circling. In their excessive attention I could read both their mistrust of these enigmas and their attraction for them. The great Dédé, narrowing his green eyes, his head on one side, was calmly enjoying himself, and saying from time to time, "It's pretty—it's pretty. It's already spoilt, but it's pretty. Next summer they'll dance because Volterra will be watching them dance."

The little gipsy Villebœuf spun round in her turn like the corolla of a flower. We refrained from speaking, dazed by the whirling and the unpleasant light. The draught of the dance drove against the ceiling a veil of smoke that tried, at every pause, to come down again, and I remember that I was content hardly to think, to accept the battered music, that year's little white wine that became tepid as soon as it was poured out, and the increasing heat heavy with smells. Coarse tobacco triumphed, then gave way to green mint, which was effaced by a rough, musty smell of clothes soaked in brine; but a brown body, sheathed in a little knitted, sleeveless jerkin, smelt as it passed of sandal wood, and the swing-door of the cellar gave out fumes of wine dripping on sand. The good shoulder of a friend propped me up and I was waiting until satiety should give me the strength and desire to get up and return to my tiny kingdom, to the anxious cats, the vines, the black mulberry trees. I was waiting for that . . . a minute more and I'll go . . . only that truly. . . .

"It's no good," said a young cinnamon-coloured woman, "what we needed this evening was Vial."

"Take me home, Hélène," I said, getting up. "You know very well that I can't drive in the dark."

I remember that she drove me very gently, avoiding the stones and the holes which are familiar to us, and that she dipped her headlights on arriving so that they would light up the path. On the way she talked of the dance, the temperature, and the little local roads in a tone so restrained, so heavy with solicitude and attentiveness that, when she ventured to ask me in a voice full of feeling, "Isn't it three years that they've left these two holes unfilled?" I was tempted to answer: "No thank you, Hélène, I don't need any cupping-glasses this evening, and the bromide potion is unnecessary."

I could tell she was full of zeal and attentions, as though she had felt on me a painless bruise and spilt blood that I didn't feel myself. It was to thank her that I said to her, when she ran to open my gate that doesn't fasten, while I was putting down my aged Brabançon bitch: "You were superb this evening, Hélène, even better than last month."

She drew herself up with pride in front of the head-lights.

"Was I? I feel it's true, Madame Colette. And it isn't over! It's only beginning. I think . . ."

She lifted her finger like a great warring angel, up-right in the middle of a white halo. Putting mystery aside, she turned her head towards the "Thimble".

"Really?" I said vaguely, and hurried along the path with a sort of repugnance for everything that wasn't my own lair, the welcome of the creatures, the cool sheets, a cavern of silence. But Hélène rushed forward and seized me by the elbow, and all I could then see in front of us was two enormous ink-blue shadows that crept along flat on the ground, were broken at the foot of the façade, scaled it vertically and gesticulated on the roof.

"Madame, it's crazy and stupid, but without the slightest reason I have a . . . a presentiment . . . like a great hope . . . Madame, I'm very devoted to you, you know . . . Madame, you understand everything. . . ."

Her long shadow gave my shorter shadow an inco-herent kiss that fell somewhere into the air, and she left me, running.

I've just been sorting some papers in dear papa's desk. I found there all the letters that I wrote to him from the Maison Dubois after my operation, and all the telegrams you sent him during the period when I couldn't write to him. He had kept everything; how moved I was! But, you'll say to me, it's quite natural that he should have kept all that. Not so natural, believe me; you'll see. When I returned from the two or three short trips I made to Paris to see you, before his death, I found my dear Colette a shadow of himself and hardly eating. Ah, what a child! What a pity he should have loved me so much! It was his love for me that destroyed, one after another, all those splendid abilities he had for literature and the sciences. He preferred to think only of me, to torment himself for me, and that was what I found inexcusable. So great a love! What frivolity! And as for my side of it, how can you expect me to get over the loss of so tender a friend?"

A gentle rain has been falling for two hours, and is about to stop. Already the heavenly bodies are disputing the end of the afternoon. A rainbow has tried to bridge the bay; broken off half-way over by a solid mass of stormy clouds, it brandishes in the air the marvellous fragment of a semicircular arch whose colours blend in death. Facing it the sun, with its

104

spokes of divergent rays, descends slowly towards the sea. The waxing moon, white in the broad daylight, frolics between wisps of airy clouds. It is the first rain of the summer. What good will it do the vintage? None. The grapes are almost ripe. When I try them at the first dawn they're cold, bedewed and elastic, spurting sweet juice as you bite into them.

The pines filter the shower as it slackens; in spite of the scent of them, of the wet orange trees and the sulphurous seaweed smoking along the shore, this water from heaven bestows on Provence a smell of mist, of undergrowth, of September, of the provinces in the centre of France. What a great rarity to find a misty horizon below my window! I see the landscape trembling, as though through rising tears. There's novelty and a sweet reversal of the normal in everything, even to the gesture of my handwriting, a gesture that for so long has belonged to the night. But I had to celebrate the rain in my own way—and besides, this week I have no taste except for what I don't much like.

The shower drifts away to *Les Maures*. All the denizens of my house celebrate the end of the bad weather. A hymn of thanksgiving, besprinkled with "Mercy me!", "Lord preserve us!" and "Jesus, I surrender!" arises from the kitchen. The she-cat, on the edge of a puddle, gathers drops of water in the hollow of her little cat's hand and watches them trickling down, just like any young girl playing with her necklace. But the tom-cat, who had forgotten rain, hasn't yet recognised it. He sits on the threshold and studies it, shivers running over his body. A vague smile begins to appear on his pure and stupid face. If the bad weather were to continue, he would be sure to cry, all beaming with complacency, "I've understood! I remember! It's raining." As for that big boneless gawk, his daughter—whom we call the Tiny One in memory of the time when she was only six weeks old—whether it rains or shines, she goes hunting. She is heavy with murders, and standoffish. Her fur, lighter coloured than it should be with blue blood like hers, is like white frost on a slate roof. A heady scent of bird's blood, trodden grass and warm lofts follows her, and her mother avoids her as though she were a fox.

I have only to remain eight days without writing, and my hand forgets how to write. For the last eight or ten days—precisely since the departure of Vial—I have had a lot to do; or it would be truer to say, I've done a great deal. I've deepened and cleaned out the party-ditch that drains the superfluous waters of winter. "I tell you, it isn't the season for that!" Divine reproaches me. Then there was weeding, hard work when the earth is hard, and the rinsing of the wicker-covered demijohns. I've also oiled the shears for the vintage and rubbed them with emery-paper. Three days of great heat kept us near the sea, and in the sea, enjoying the cool weight of its short swell. A hoar frost of fine salt covered our arms and legs before they were barely dry. But although the sun attacks and overcomes us, we feel he is no longer aiming at us from the same quarters of the sky. At dawn, in front of my window, it is no longer the eucalyptus that divides the first segment of the sun rising from the sea, it is a pine next to the eucalyptus. How many of us see the day appear? The ageing of the sun, which each morning shortens its course, takes place in private. It is enough for my Parisian comrades, and for the Parisians who are not my comrades, that when it sets it should fill the sky for a long time, taking possession of the afternoon and crowning it.

Shall I tell of the two excursions that saw us, numerous and gay, happy to set off and happier to return? I love the old Provençal villages clinging to the crests of their hills. Ruins there are dry, wholesome, stripped of grass and green mildew, and only the geranium-ivy with its pink flowers hangs from the black gaping ear of a tower. But in summer I quickly tire of penetrating inland; I am thirsty for the sea, for the unwavering horizontal join, blue against blue.

I think that's all. Do you think it isn't much? Perhaps you're right. Perhaps I'm incapable of portraying for you what I myself don't clearly distinguish. Sometimes I take for silence what is a great internal rustling, weariness and happiness, and what draws a smile from me is nearly always a regret. Since Vial's departure I strive hard to attain serenity, and naturally I only bring to the task materials of sound origin, some taken from a still recent past, others from my present which is becoming clear, and the best I beg from you, my very dear. The result is that my serenity, which I've acquired without having any natural tendency, has the look—not so much artificial as painstaking—of something that's been worked at too conscientiously. I would exhort it, "Come on now, get drunk! Stagger a bit!" if I were certain that it would be merry in its cups.

When Vial was here, during two consecutive summers, his presence . . . No, if I were to speak of him I shouldn't do it well. I leave it to you, my subtle companion, to praise a Vial you have not known.

"I leave you to go and play chess with my little wool-seller. You know him. It's that ugly little fat man who sells buttons and darning-wool sadly all day long, and never says a word. But would you believe it, he plays a subtle game of chess. We play in his back-shop where there is a stove, an armchair he brings forward for me, and on the window, that gives on to a little court, two pots of very beautiful geraniums, those incomprehensible geraniums that you find in poor dwellings and in the houses of level-crossing keepers. I've never been able to have any like them, I who give them air and pure water, and pander to their every whim. So I go very often to play chess with my little wool-seller. He waits for me faithfully. He asks me each time if I want a cup of tea, because I am 'a lady' and tea is a distinguished drink. We play and I think of what is imprisoned in that fat little man. Who will ever know? It makes me curious. But I have to resign myself to

*never knowing, though I'm very glad to feel sure there's
something, and to be the only one to know it."*

Flair, instinct for hidden treasure. Like a diviner she
went straight to what shines only in secret, water which
languishes far from the light, the dormant seam, hearts
from which every chance of blossoming has been with-
drawn. She listened to the liquid sob, the long under-
ground whisper, the sigh.

She would never have asked brutally: "So, Vial,
you've become attached to me?" Such words wither
everything. Have I regrets, then? That ordinary youth?
There are no distinctions in love. Does one ask a
hero: "Little wool-seller, do you love me?" Does one
push things to their conclusion with such haste as that?
When, as a little girl, I used to get up at about seven
o'clock, astonished to find the sun still low, the swallows still perched in a line on the gutter and the nut-
tree gathering its icy shadow beneath it, I would hear
my mother cry: "Seven o'clock! My goodness, how late
it is!" Shall I never catch her up, then? Free, and flying
high, she says of constant, exclusive love, "What frivolity!" and then scorns to explain herself at length. It's
for me to understand. I do what I can. It's high time for
me to approach her by some other means than through
my professed liking for jobs without urgency or great-
ness, and to get beyond what we irreverent children
used once upon a time to call "the cult of the little blue
saucepan". She would not be satisfied—nor am I—to
know that I often gaze at and caress everything that
passes through my hands. At other times I find I am
being pushed out of my own self and forced to grant
a large measure of hospitality to those who, having
handed on to me their place on earth, are only in
appearance submerged by death. The wave of fury that
rises in me and masters me like a pleasure of the senses:
that is my father, his white Italian hand closing round
the sprung dagger that never left him, and feeling for
its blades. My father, again, is the jealousy that made

me, in other days, so awkward. I tread obediently in the footsteps, stopped for ever, that traced their way from the garden path to the cellar, from the cellar to the pump, from the pump to the big armchair full of cushions, opened books and papers. On that trodden path, lit by a low, sweeping sunbeam, the first of the day, I hope to learn why one must never put a single question to the little wool-seller—I mean to say Vial, but it is the same perfect lover—why the true name of love, that suppresses and condemns everything around it, is "frivolity".

I remember one evening—it will soon be eight days ago and it was the evening when Hélène brought me back from the dance—when I thought I had left on the road, in the arms of Hélène's shadow clasping the shoulders of my shadow, a relic that was not exactly meant for her but which it was important that I should get rid of—old reflexes, servitudes, harmless aberrations.

When Hélène had gone I opened the door of the enclosure giving on to the vineyard, and called my creatures: "My creatures!" They rushed up, bathed in moonlight, impregnated with the odours that they get from the beads of resin and the hairy mints, deified by the night, and once again I was amazed that, being so beautiful and so free, masters of themselves and of those night hours, they should prefer to come running at my voice.

Then I settled the bitch in an open drawer of the chest-of-drawers and installed in front of me, on my bed, the low table with its rubber *sabots,* adjusted the porcelain shade whose green light answered, from afar, the red lamp that Vial lit in the "Thimble".

"You are the starboard light, and I the port side," jested Vial.

"Yes," I answered, "we never look towards each other."

Then I took the top off the softened gold nib of one

of my fountain-pens, the one that runs best, and I did not write. I let the night, the long night, minister to me. The next night, and the next, will be longer still. Nights, like bodies, stretch themselves as the fever of summer leaves them. And I said to myself that, as far as the décor was concerned—the black night, the solitude, the friendly animals, a great circle of fields and sea all around—I should be thenceforward like the woman I have described many a time, that solitary upright woman like a sad rose which carries itself the more proudly for having been stripped of its leaves. But I no longer trust in what I look like, having known the time when, while I was painting this lonely creature, I would go to show my lie, page by page, to a man, asking him, "Have I lied well?" And I would laugh, as my forehead sought that man's shoulder, and his ear that I nibbled, for I could never get over the belief that I had lied. Nibbling the cool gristly lobe of his ear and pressing his shoulder, I laughed under my breath. "You're there, aren't you?" But already all that I held was a deceptive solidity. Why did he stay? I inspired him with confidence. He knew I could be left alone with matches, the gas, and firearms.

The gate sang. On the path, where the water shed by the sky smokes as it weds the warm earth, a young woman is walking towards my house, shaking, as she passes, the great weeping plumage of the mimosas. It is Hélène. Since Vial's departure she no longer joins us at the morning bathe where she meets, in spite of my protection, some cold faces, for I count among my friends some beings of a redoubtable simplicity, who are bad at understanding the sound of words because their task is to hear the passage of thoughts.

Hélène is soon leaving for Paris. When I announced this news, only the little voice of Morhange answered me. "Ah, so much the better, that gawk! I don't like her, she isn't good."

I pressed for the reason of such a lively antipathy.

"No, she isn't good," said Morhange. "And the proof is that I don't like her."

With evening a great wind arose. It has dried the rain, carrying away the clouds, swollen like big soft water-skins, bringers of benign humidity. It's blowing from the north, telling of dryness, of distant snow, of a tense, invisible season already installed up there on the Alps.

The animals sit and gravely watch it endlessly passing beyond the black window. Perhaps they are thinking of winter. This is the first evening when we've gathered in a closer circle. The cats were waiting for me under the penthouse of reeds when I got in. I had dined with my neighbours opposite, a young couple who are building their nest with religious gravity. They are still so thrilled with their new possessions that I hurry to leave them alone, so that when I've gone they can count over again the treasures they have acquired, and timidly talk of the things they quiver with longing to possess. After dinner in their house an empty cradle is brought into the low hall with its ceiling of great beams; this is filled with a little child as round and pink as a radish, made to fit it. Then I know that it is ten o'clock, and I go home.

Hélène did not stay long this afternoon. She came to tell me that she was taking the road, as she puts it, in her five-horse-power car, with a friend who can take turns with her at the wheel and change a tire.

"Vial never leaves Paris, Madame Colette. He's working like a dog at his big undertaking for the *Quatre Quartiers*. . . . I have my spies," she added.

"Not too many spies, Hélène, not too many spies."

"Don't be afraid! My spies means father, and he's helping Vial with little tips. Vial will need father, next winter, if the Ministry doesn't fall, because father's a school-friend of the Minister's. The important thing is that the *Quatre Quartier* should make Vial director of their workshops before the Ministry falls."

She shook hands with me and a word of passion escaped her: "Ah, Madame, I should so love to help him!"

She will get Vial. I've tried, these last days, to urge on her prudence in pursuit—"dignity" and not "prudence" was what I had in mind—and a different strategical style. But she swept my advice aside with a wide gesture of her bare arm, and tossed her head with great confident tosses. So it was quite evident that I knew nothing about it. She has a way that is tender and proud of saying to me, "Don't be afraid!" For two pins she would add, "Now that you're no longer in the neighbourhood of Vial, I can deal with him."

For two or three weeks past I've sometimes taken pride in the thought that, if I wanted to do harm, I could. "I could still make do with that," Vial had said, craftily. We were both boasting. Hélène will get Vial and that will be right—my hand nearly wrote: and it will serve her right?

It's blowing outside, but without a drop of rain. I shall lose the rest of my pears in it, but the laden vines laugh at the mistral. *"I wonder whether you've inherited my love for tempests and all the disasters of nature?"* wrote my mother to me. No. The wind, as a rule, chills my thoughts, turning me away from the present and back along the one-way street of the past. But this evening the present does not link up comfortably with my past. Since Vial left I have once again to be patient, to go forward without looking back, and only face-about deliberately, in six months, or three weeks. What, so many precautions? Yes, so many precautions, and dread of all haste, and a slow chemistry; I must cherish the sources of my memories.

One day I shall find myself savouring the love in my past, and I shall be astonished at the great troubles, the battles, the feasts, the solitudes. Bitter April, with its feverish wind, its bees caught on the sticky brown ɪds, its scent of apricot trees in flower will bring the spring itself to salute me, just as it was when it burst into my life, dancing, weeping, mad and wounded by its own thorns. But perhaps I shall think: "I've had better. I've had Vial."

You will be astonished: "What, that little man, who said three words and went away? Really, that little man, to dare to compare him with . . ." It's not a thing one can argue about. When one praises the beauty of one of her daughters to a mother, she smiles to herself because she thinks it is the ugly one who is the prettiest. I'm not singing Vial's praises in any lyrical vein, I merely regret him. Yes, I regret him. The need to exalt him will only come when I begin to regret him less. He'll come down to earth again—when my memory has finished its capricious work, that often removes a monster's hump or horn, effaces a mountain and respects a straw, an antenna, a reflection—he'll come down and take his place in the depths to which love, that superficial froth, does not always have access.

Then I shall think of him, telling myself once again that I let him go, that I gave Vial to a young woman with a gesture which undoubtedly had a wonderful air of ostentation and recklessness. Already, if I reread what I wrote nearly three weeks ago, I find I painted Vial badly there, with a precision which impoverishes his outline. During these past days I've thought a lot about Vial. To-day I'm thinking much more about myself, since I'm regretting him. O dear Man, our difficult friendship is still unsure of itself, thank heaven!

Let me cry once more, "Thank heaven!" my very dear mother. It's done, now I'll be quiet. It's for you to bid me be silent again. So speak on the verge of death, speak in the name of your inflexible standards, in the name of the unique virtue that you called "true elegance of behaviour".

"All right then, I deceived you, in order to have peace. Old Josephine is not sleeping in the little house. I sleep there alone. Spare me, all of you! Don't come

and tell me, you and your brother, stories of burglars and wicked tramps. As far as nocturnal visitors are concerned, there's only one that must cross my threshold now, as you well know. Give me a dog, if you want. Yes, a dog, I'll agree to that. But don't compel me to be shut up with someone at night! I've reached the point where I can't bear to have a human being sleeping in my house, when it's a human being I haven't made myself. My own code of morals won't let me. It's the final return to single life when you refuse to have any longer in your house, especially if it's a small one, an unmade bed, a pail of slops, an individual—man or woman—walking about in a night-shirt. Ugh! No, no, no more company at night, no more strangers breathing, no more of that humiliation of waking up simultaneously! I prefer to die, it's more seemly.

"And having made my choice, I'm all for coquetry. You remember that, at the time of my operation, I had two big bed-jackets made for me, in white flannel? I've just had a single one made out of the two of them. What for? Why, to be buried in. It has a hood, trimmed with lace all round, real thread lace—you know how it gives me the creeps to touch cotton lace. The same lace on the sleeves and round the collar (there's a collar). Precautions of this kind are part of my feeling for what's right and proper. I'm already upset enough that Victor Considérant should have felt obliged to give my sister-in-law Caro a magnificent ebony coffin, with silver handles, that he had had made to measure for his own wife. But she was so swollen she couldn't get into it. That silly creature, Caro, appalled by such a present, gave it to her charwoman. Why didn't she give it to me? I like luxury, and can't you see how comfortably lodged I should have been in it? Don't let this letter upset you, it comes when it should and is what it ought to be.

"How many more games of chess have I still before me? For I still play, from time to time, with my little wool-seller. Nothing is changed, except that now

*it's I who play less well than he, and who lose. When
I become too incapable and clumsy, I shall give that
up as I give up everything else, out of decency."*

It's good to learn such a lesson of behaviour. What
breeding! I think I hear her, and pull myself together.
Fly, my favourite! Don't reappear until you have become unrecognisable. Jump through the window and,
as you touch the ground, change, blossom, fly, resound. . . . You could deceive me twenty times before
you imposed on her, but all the same serve your sentence, slough off your skin. When you return to me
I must be able to give you, as my mother did, your
name of "pink cactus" or some other flame-shaped
flower that uncloses painfully, the name you will acquire when you have been exorcised.

She wrote the letter that I have just copied with a
hand that was still free. Her pointed nibs scratched the
paper—she always made a great noise as she wrote.
That letter, written to protect herself—and us—from
imprisonment, illness and immodesty, must have filled
her room with a scraping noise like the frantic feet of
an insect. Yet at the end of the lines the last words
turn down, drawn by an invisible slope. Brave though
she was, she is afraid. She is thinking with dread of
being dependent, of dependence in general; and she
takes the trouble to warn me. The next day in another
letter she delicately changed the subject to relieve my
mind: a charming story of some wild oats, whose
beards, thrusting to right or left, foretell the weather,
follows her previous admonitions. She grows enthusi-
astic in relating the visit of her grand-daughter G,
during one of her bad fits of drowsiness, when she was
drugged with *digitalis*.

*"Eight years old, her black locks all tangled, for she
had run to bring me a rose. She remained on the threshold of my room, as alarmed by my waking as by my
sleep. I shall see nothing before my death as beautiful*

as that shy child, who wanted to cry and held out a rose." Between us two, which is the better writer, she or I? Does it not resound to high heaven that it is she?

Dawn comes, the wind falls. From yesterday's rain, in the shade, a new perfume is born; or is it I who am once again going to discover the world and apply new senses to it? It's not too much to be born and to create each day. The bronze-coloured hand that runs, stops, crosses out and starts again, is cold with emotion, cold with a youthful emotion. For hadn't niggardly love wanted to fill my cupped hands one last time with a little shrivelled treasure? In future I shall gather nothing except by armfuls. Great armfuls of wind, of coloured atoms, of generous emptiness that I shall dump down proudly on the threshing floor.

Dawn comes. Everyone knows that no demon can stand its approach, its pallor, its bluish gliding; but no one ever speaks of the translucent demons that amorously attend upon it. A blue of farewells, choked and spread by the mist, billows fog-like into the room. I need but little sleep; for many weeks now I have made do with a siesta. When the desire for sleep seizes me again, I shall sleep the brutal sleep of a drunkard. I have only to wait for the return of a rhythm interrupted for a time. Only to wait, to wait. . . . That is a lesson learnt in a good school, where true elegance of manners is taught also, the supreme elegance of knowing how to diminish.

I learn it from you, to whom I turn without ceasing. A letter, the last, came quickly after the laughing epistle about the ebony coffin. Ah, let me hide under that last letter the image that I don't want to see: a head half vanquished, turning its dry neck impatiently from side to side on the pillow, like a poor goat tethered too short. No doubt my mother wrote that last letter to assure me that she no longer felt any obligation to use our language. Two pencilled sheets have on them nothing more than apparently joyful signs, arrows emerging from an embryo word, little rays, "yes, yes" together, and a single "she danced", very clear. Lower down she had written "my treasure"—her name for me when our separations had lasted a long time and she was longing to see me again. But this time I feel a scruple in claiming for myself so burning a word. It has a place among strokes, swallow-like interweavings, plant-like convolutions—all messages from a hand that was trying to transmit to me a new alphabet or the sketch of some ground-plan envisaged at dawn under rays that would never attain the sad zenith. So that instead of a confused delirium, I see in that letter one of those haunted landscapes where, to puzzle you, a face lies hidden among the leaves, an arm in the fork of a tree, a body under a cluster of rock.

The cold blue has crept into my bedroom, trailing after it a very faint tinge of flesh colour that clouds it. It is the dawn, wrested from the night, drenched and chill. The same hour to-morrow will find me cutting the first grapes of the vintage. The day after to-morrow, even before this hour, I want . . . Not so fast! Not so fast! That deep hunger for the moment which gives birth to the day must learn patience: the ambiguous friend who leapt through the window is still wandering about. He did not put off his shape as he touched the ground. He has not had time enough to perfect himself. But I only have to help him and lo! he will turn into a quickset hedge, spindrift, meteors, an open and unending book, a cluster of grapes, a ship, an oasis. . . .

ABOUT THE AUTHOR

Sidonie Gabrielle Colette (1873–1954) was one of the most famous and honored French writers of this century. The first woman member of The Academie Goncourt, a holder of the Grand Cross of the Legion of Honor, she was also the first woman in French history to be granted a state funeral.

Colette began her writing career in collaboration with Willy, her husband. In 1900, when she was twenty-seven, Colette's first novel, *Claudine at School*, was published and became a sensational success. During the next few years, several *Claudine* books followed. After divorcing Willy, Colette earned her living as a music-hall mime, and in 1907, her first independent novel appeared, *Retreat from Love*.

With the outbreak of World War I, Colette began a career as a special correspondent in Rome and Venice and as a contributor to *Le Matin*, a leading Paris daily. Her journalism included dramatic criticism, law-court reporting, and sketches of contemporary life. During this time, Colette continued to write novels.

During her last years, Colette, crippled by arthritis and confined to her Paris apartment, wrote reminiscences and descriptive works that gained her new renown. Before her death in 1954, at the age of eighty-one, Colette had written more than fifty books and was best known as the creator of *Gigi*, *Cheri* and *The Last of Cheri*, and the *Claudine* novels. Her place in twentieth-century fiction is comparable among her countrymen only with that of Proust.

Books by Colette to be published by Ballantine are: *The Vagabond*, *The Shackle*, *Cheri* and *The Last of Cheri*, *Claudine at School*, *Claudine in Paris*, *Claudine Married* and *Claudine and Annie*, *Break of Day*, and *Letters from Colette*.